Margaret J Carr

Teresa's War

Editions Dedicaces

TERESA'S WAR

Published by:
   Editions Dedicaces LLC
   12759 NE Whitaker Way, Suite D833
   Portland, Oregon, 97230
   www.dedicaces.us

Library of Congress Cataloging-in-Publication Data
   Carr, Margaret J
   Teresa's War /
   by Margaret J Carr.
   p. cm.
   ISBN-13: 978-1-77076-443-9 (alk. paper)
   ISBN-10: 1-77076-443-7 (alk. paper)

Margaret J Carr

Teresa's War

A previously untold story of extraordinary bravery. The central character's names have been changed to protect their identities and privacy, and there is no direct reference to the relevant places. Although this is based on the true facts, other characters and events have been created to complete the story.

MARGARET J CARR

Foreword

November 11th and it was a cold, crisp day, but it was dry and a much welcomed respite from the strong winds and rain that had seen October out and the first ten days of the new month in. The old woman, Mrs Teresa Hunt, welcomed such days as she slowly walked beneath the tree branches now almost striped of their autumn spectacle.

She had reached the familiar small square park with tall elegant houses on two sides and roads bordering the others. It was criss-crossed with narrow paths lined with grass and weeds, and tall old trees. At the central paved roundel where the paths met, two worn wooden benches faced one another. Dropping her heavy plastic carrier bags on the damp, muddy ground, she sat on the one facing the busy road and eased her swollen right foot out of the utilitarian lace-up shoe. She wriggled her toes, twisted and deformed by the advancing arthritis. The east wind, blowing straight in her face, was cold, but it helped to reminded her of a place she hadn't seen in sixty years and was becoming increasingly harder to recall. Her memory was gradually fading and it frightened her. Only last week she had walked to the town and looked down to find she was still wearing her bedroom slippers. Days later she had put the light on under an empty pan on the cooker. She'd not realized until the smoke filled her tiny home. But more than anything she was sad that one day she might forget her early years back home.

There was a sharp biting chill and she pulled her woolen hat down over her ears.

Had she remembered everything? She hoped so. She'd somehow lost her carefully printed shopping-list, probably somewhere between the cenotaph and the supermarket. She knew her neighbour could be quite sharp and she'd be angry if she'd forgotten something of hers. Teresa glanced with a worried frown, down at the shopping bags sprawled at her feet. Had she forgotten anything?

It worried her and the thought played over and over in her mind. Was her month's rent due tomorrow or next week, or had she already paid it? The idea she might have missed the date filled her with fear and dread. She was frightened of her landlord, so ready to shout at her and call her stupid, because she was a foreigner in his country, and she didn't want him suddenly arriving on her door step waving his arms about because she was in arrears. She had always paid on time, and was never behind with her rent or any bills, but then up to recently she'd been able to remember such important things.

She sat back against the worn wooden slats and half closed her eyes, thankful that, weather permitting and providing it wasn't pouring with rain, or snowing and icy under foot, she always liked to stop right here on this bench to rest before continuing on her journey. It was another half mile trudge to her small rented, two bed roomed terraced house a few streets away, and the park was probably about a third of the way home. Teresa didn't like to admit it to herself but the weekly trip was becoming harder, her old bones protested more than ever. Now pushing the fingers of one hand through the gap between the buttons in her warm coat and under the thick wrapping of a scarf, she rubbed at the sudden sharp twinge that occasional caught her unawares, making it hard to breath for a few frightening seconds. But then, just as suddenly, it would subside and almost disappear leaving behind a residue of an acceptable ache.

The Remembrance Service, at the town's cenotaph was something the old woman never missed whatever the weather or temperature, not even the year she'd had that nasty dose of flu only the week before and it had left her feeling weak and vulnerable right up to Christmas.

This morning her next door neighbour had caught Teresa on her way out. Knowing her routine, she also knew that after the solemn ceremony, Teresa would call in at the supermarket on the main street before making her way home.

Gloria Riley, was only a few years her junior, yet still imagined herself a young desirable woman. She was thin and shapeless, a faded beauty, but with a propensity to live in her own narcissi bubble.

It had once been a life to all intense and purpose, very ordinary and mundane until she'd meant her gentleman friend ten years before. He had changed her life from mundane to one of glamour and glitz, dinner parties and business functions and, needing a companion and escort for these factions, Gloria fit the bill. He was only too happy to provide the necessary clothes, hair-dos and regular facials to attend these in style. Money was no object. And on occasion his function companion loved to show her appreciation with intimate home-cooked meals.

That morning, in her dressing gown, smoking her third cigarette and sipping the mug of latte, she was seated on the bright pink brocade-covered settee peering through the frou-frou lace curtained window. She was eager to catch her neighbour as she opened her own front door next to hers. Ms Riley, as she expected Teresa to call her, rushed down the narrow hallway and out through the door as soon as she heard the recognizable creaking of old hinges.

'Teresa. Teresa dear,' she all but pounced on the startled woman. 'If you wouldn't mind I've got something I need pressing and you do such a good job with the iron.' It was always said in that patronizing *I'm better than you* way she had.

'If you'd do it now, I can be showering and getting dressed. It won't take you more than a mo. You'll be popping into the supermarket and there are a few things I could do with. Would you mind? I know you'll be going to the cenotaph first, but I don't mind that.'

Teresa hadn't minded. She never did: perhaps because at least, now nearly eighty, someone, anyone still needed her. She never thought of herself as subservient and so followed the neighbour inside her chintzy, over-filled house. They went through to the kitchen and Teresa walked over to the readily set-up ironing board and a basket filled with crumpled items. She didn't say a word as she began her chore and Ms Riley say back on a chair at her dining table, smoked a cigarette and told her of her date later that day. She reiterated again and again the importance of the luxury items of food she'd need later.

'I've just a few odds and ends I need in a hurry for my dinner party this evening, and I simply haven't time to go to the shops before my personal hairdresser arrives. She's so good with my hair it'll need a tint. I knew you'd come to my rescue.'

She said this in an unnecessarily loud and forced posh voice to emphasize her own importance and making sure, that in her world, the old Austrian woman knew her place.

Teresa nodded as if these roles were normal. A lady and her servant.

Gloria Riley never told anyone the truth regarding her early life. As the fifth child of parents who both drank, rowed and fought loudly they lived on a rough, rundown council estate. In reality, Gloria had had little schooling, but nevertheless had learnt the important life-lessons mainly on the streets close to home. There she had used her youthful beauty to flirt and tempt towards a better future and get away from her roots. And it had paid off. She'd moved to this town and after a string of mundane low-paid work finally met this gentleman friend and her life had changed overnight.

Everything about the woman Gloria had changed. She'd soon started to exhibit the airs and graces of a woman of substance. In reality Ms Riley lived on benefits, her furniture was made up of flat packs and her 'designer' clothes she bought on her fortnightly trip to a market stall.

But Teresa knew none of this, and it's doubtful it would have made any difference if she had. Teresa always tried to please others and if it meant picking up a carton of cream, eggs, cheese and asparagus so Ms Riley could entertain her gentleman friend, then she would. He was an Important Person in the town, or so Gloria Riley continually informed Teresa as she primped and preened. Teresa Hunt carefully pressed Ms Riley garment.

'That blouse was very expensive dear. It's very fragile so be careful you don't snag the material. I'm going to wear it this evening.'

Being as careful as she could be, Teresa pressed the delicate material until it was to her neighbour's satisfaction.

'Oh, and while the ironing boards up and you're here, could you iron that skirt and dress, and the pillowcases and duvet at the bottom of the basket,' adding with a certain girlish coyness, 'I'd better change my bed later.'

The shopping list was handed to Teresa as she stepped from the house and hurried on her way to the cenotaph. Later she'd bought her neighbour's items along with her own bag of potatoes, carrots and onions to which she would add lentils and herbs to make a savoury, tasty stew in a big pan on the stove. It was all quite heavy, but she told herself her shoulders were strong and she didn't really mind. It was good to buy all these vegetables and by adding more, and extra stock, she would have enough to see her over many days. The meals helped to reminded her of mother and her native country and as she sat very still until the pain in her chest shifted, she sighed with a heartfelt, yet nowadays rare, nostalgia.

She sat with a growing sense she really should be on her way, but the autumn sun was warm on her face and it wouldn't harm to stay for a few more minutes. Her neighbour would probably get quite *shirty* if she was kept waiting. *Shirty*, Teresa loved that word. Her memory might be going and her body stiffening and it wasn't always easy to recall Ernest's gentle face without looking at their black and white wedding photo she always kept beside her bed or the tiny image in her locket, but s*hirty,* it was one of the English slang words he'd had taught her during their many years of happy marriage. She missed him so much, even after all these years alone. Her life wouldn't have been so lonely if he and Emily were still here. If their only child had not been taken, she may even have had grandchildren now. But in her own way Teresa Hunt was philosophical, this was the way things were and she could do nothing to change them. Although there were many times when Ms Riley's snappy, patronizing manner might bring a tear to the old woman's eye at least she was a constant form of company in an otherwise lonely life., and was glad at least someone valued her in a world that was getting more strange and puzzling by the day. She was confused and alarmed by its modern ways. What would *Mutti und Vater* have thought of this internet, computer age that seemed to inhibit children's innocence?

Unconsciously she fingered the red fabric poppy pinned to her lapel, and moved her back against the wooden slats. She watched a few people strolling by enjoying the rays of weak sunlight filtering through the trees. There was a young woman, no more than a child herself, with a baby in a buggy, carting bags from the supermarket. A man let his dog off the lead to run free, as an elderly couple strolling arm in arm nodded as they passed by.

Down the side road vehicles drove to turn into the main road and hardly disturbed the chorus of birds high in the branches, or the relaxing tranquility of this square oasis in the centre of the busy town.

For the old woman it was a few moments to let her mind wander back in time to another place, another land.

Teresa half closed her eyes and relaxed as she was transported back, in that corner of her memory that remained sharp and poignant, to the small family farm she had grown up on. Sadly it was a land she'd never see again. The Austrian Tyrol with its rolling hills and deep valleys, thick forests and the clear alpine air. She could almost smell the scent of summertime wild flowers and hear the bleating of the goats that they kept on the farm and roamed the hills.

It had been a mix of normality and a dark, threatening menace that had invaded the very countryside and changed her life forever.

Chapter I

Hilde and Josef Gőetschl, and their two daughters lived in on the outskirts of a small sprawling town in the Tyrol. It nestled in a valley beneath rolling hills, natural meadows and the distant grey snow-peaked mountains to the north. To the southwest and beyond the thick, woods and tall, closely packed pine forest was the border to the next country as close as two kilometers away.

Their eldest Teresa had been born in March in 1935, her sister Liesl two years later, in the small chalet house. The girls took after their mother in looks. Both sturdy in build with rosy cheeks, above full laughing mouths and eyes the colour of hazelnuts. Although Hilde's light brown hair was worn in braids curved around her small neat head, her daughter's wore theirs in long plaits almost long enough to sit on.

Their father Josef was slight in build, a shadow of the strong muscular young man Hilde had married in the spring of thirty three. His once thick, mahogany brown hair was thinning and hung in wispy strands hardly framing his pale, thin face. The cough that often wracked his emaciated body, made the sinews in his neck stand out like knotted rope and the hollows in his cheeks more pronounced with every attack.

The rear of their small home, facing west, was tucked against the base of the hill that rose gently towards the deep blue of the Tyrolean sky in a gentle grass and wild flowered covered slope. Over the summit and it swept down into large open grassland and then swathes of forest and thick woodland. Beyond, the first of the mountain range reared above as dense, rocks with deep, hidden crevices that

15

hardly ever lost the lingering snow even in the height of summer. In the shimmering heat-haze it was an illusion the mountains were much closer.

Without fear Teresa, her sister and mother would often search the forest floor for wild berries, mushrooms, wild herbs and garlic, until it became an environment nearly as familiar to them as the walk each day to the school room and small church nestling in the next valley.

But Teresa had never ventured beyond the forest's farthest perimeter, stopping at the edge of the stretch of land and course ground with the mountains beyond. Instead she would listen in wonder as her father told of when his best friend Hans and he were in their teens, they'd cycled miles skirting the forest on their pushbikes to the narrow pass between the mountains and climbed a neighbouring Swiss mountain almost to the peak. It wasn't a very high mountain but there they'd breathed in air that was so sharp and biting it seemed to scorch their lungs. They were able to see further than they could ever have imagined: to far distant mist-covered mountains, deep unseen valleys and dense lines of dark forests and beyond to other lands. They'd felt as if they were standing on the top of the world. Teresa had wondered at the image: what would it be like to stand on the very top of the world? Her father had taken that journey only once in his youth. In fact he had never again left the valley and the town nestling beneath the hills. Now he barely left their small chalet except to walk the short distance into the town and the Heurigen to meet his friends and drink wine.

The single storey chalet with its one large room, set on the small plot of land, was adequate for the needs of the family.

Mutti, vater, Teresa und Leisl.

There was nothing she'd enjoyed more than running free amongst tall grass and rolling hills, and hiding in the clump of trees and bushes bordering their small plot of land or exploring deep within the mighty forest. She'd always felt safe.

But it wasn't all playtime, she'd had her own chores to do and at seven Teresa collected the eggs from the scattering of hens that pecked and clucked in the dust outside the door, the honking line of geese, the goats Gertrude and Matilda needed milking and with their kids taken to the hill to roam. She helped her mother to pull the carrots, cabbages and other seasonal vegetables from their small garden and she also helped to tend to her father's needs.

Her poor *Vater*.

He was sick man, unable to work because of a weak chest that meant for days or even weeks he had a terrible hacking cough and the victim of fierce, strength-sapping convulsions. Those meant he was frequently confined to spending days in the large double bed with its comfortable feather mattress in the bed cupboard in the far wall. There he'd lay head against the pillows, his eyes closed with the increasing tightening pain in his chest and smoke one or two of his soothing cigarettes, until gradually the pain would ease.

The double pine doors could be closed together when not in use. The single large room, taking up almost the entire floor space also housed the large pine table and chairs, the kitchen range with the shelves and dresser and the settle that also doubled as the girls bed during the long, cold winters.

It was the summer months Teresa liked best, when the two girls slept in the big comfortable bed under the eaves. Through the pane of glass in the sloping roof Leisl and Theresa could see the arc of clear navy-blue, scattered with the multitude of shining stars, then watch as the first rays of sun beckoned a new day. Teresa would get herself and her young sister dressed for breakfast but before the lovely thick porridge, she would have to feed the noisy, bad-tempered geese that roamed the small yard in the back and the hens that appeared expectantly from the tumbledown shed against the far wall off the chalet. There was always the eggs to collect, brown and large, the rich yolks the colour of the sun on a hot summer's day, the goats and the geese. All chores had to be completed before Teresa, Leisl and *Mutty* walked to the church for early service three times a week and the girls would walk along the lane to join the other children for lessons in the school room.

Teresa enjoyed school. The lessons taught were more than the basic reading, writing and adding up sums. The children all liked their teacher he was kind and thoughtful, and talked of interesting things.

As she sat, an old woman in her adopted land, alone and lonely on that November day over seventy years later Teresa struggled to recall her teacher's narrative. She wanted to imagine she could hear him now, so clear and enthusiastic that it was as if he was talking in her head.

To his eager students Albert Grassinger seemed old, but was probably in his forties. He had never married but lived with his widowed mother in the house he'd been born in. He was a tall, thin man with just a fine ridge of dark hair around a bald spot, large fleshy ears that often mesmerized Teresa the way they tended to stick out and glow red when he stood with his back against the light cast by the high window. He had a prominent beak nose with dark nose hairs, but above all he had soft, gentle eyes that sparkled with humour. She looked forward to the stories Herr Grassinger read to them from his row of books sitting in the bookcase behind his high desk. To Teresa the many coloured spines shone like jewels, their innards filled with stories of adventures and glory: other times and different people, magical castles in faraway places. There had been so many tales that left her breathless with anticipation and eager to hear more. Occasionally Herr Grassinger would settle a lean buttock on the edge of his high desk to talk of the many varied places he'd visited in his lifetime, the people and their cultures. He had a large coloured globe that

18

he used, to point to exotic, mystical lands. He drew pictures in the young girl's mind of India with its overpowering heat, sudden monsoons, heavy scents of rich spices and the bustling sounds of busy Bombay with such a wealth of people it was impossible to imagine. And America with its vast diversity of cultures and cities, wild open dusty plains that were home to many dangerous animals and insects, and, not unlike their own land, the high mountain ranges clothed in thick forests that were the homes of deer and elk, gorges deep and skies so large they stretched wide there the predatorily condors and eagles swooped and searched the ground for tasty morsels. He spoke of the oceans and seas so deep, and vast that seemed to go on forever. She'd never seen the sea, only the fast flowing rivers close to her home, so it was hard to imagine so much water.

She was so filled with the wonders of the world, she daily skipped home to the small chalet on the side of the hill eager to tell *Vater* everything she'd learned as he lay sick and weak in the bed in the cupboard.

Their mother worked hard. Apart from cooking and cleaning for her family, she cultivated the small patch of earth fenced off at the side of their chalet, in which she grew all manner of tasty vegetables and herbs for the pot, making the most of the each season's bounty.

Teresa's mother was a skilled needlewoman, having been taught by her mother, who had learnt the craft from her mother before her. She was the family's main source of income taking in the sewing from the ladies in the nearby town. She made the best: almost invisible hand stitching dresses, shirts, mending and patching the numerous garments often by an oil lamp far into the night.

Deeply religious, Hilde Göetschl and her daughters attended the tiny church each week. They would make their way through lush fields and over the small rise of the hill to genuflect, kneel, and bow their heads fingering their rosary to thank Jesus for another day.

'Always remember *leibchen*,' Hilde preached daily to her daughters. 'Jesus will look after us.'

Leisl was too young to fully understand, was content to play with the rosary beads as her mother prayed.

It had been a happy, carefree life because she knew no other. Teresa recalled, as if it was only yesterday, how her mother's smile always made every scrape of knee or stomach ache better. She made all their clothes, and the young girls loved the colourful, matching cotton dresses for summer and the thick woolen blouses and skirts for the harsh winters.

Teresa was saddened and scared on the many occasions when her father struggled to breathe during a bad attack of coughing. But what seemed even worse was the times his eyes would roll back into his head revealing the greyish blue-veined whites and his body would convulse and stiffen, twitch and jerk uncontrollably. It was these times when the girls saw their mother very gently hold his head and sooth him until the seizures ended. Only then, with the help of her eldest, Hilde would carry him to the bed in the cupboard and after laying him on the soft duck down mattress, kiss his brow and leave him to sleep a deep calming sleep.

However the fits frightened and confused Leisl. She would hide in the falling down barn, amongst the straw, or up in the roof space nursing her wooden dolly whittled made by her father. *Mutti* had dressed it in a frock made from the scraps left over from a skirt for Clara Mueller, and an underskirt made from material used to turn the cuffs on the butcher's work shirt. It was her favourite toy and went everywhere with her. Of course she didn't understand what was happening to her father but quickly forgot as she played happily on the hand pegged rug or chased the hens around the yard.

But thankfully there where the times when Josef was well enough to sit out in the sun, fashioning a piece of kindling or wood into a whistle or the figure of an animal. During the harsh winter he'd lovingly made a three legged stool to stand in the nook at the side of the fire. And there were also the times when, after his wife handed him a few coins left over from her latest dress-making work, and he would walk slowly into the town and the Heurigen to spend time with his friends, Hans Schultz, Felix Hofler the bank manager, Bernie Winkler the pawnbroker and the self elected mayor cum police chief Henrich Mueller. Sometimes Teresa, sharing the couch to one side of the room with her sister, or the double bed beneath the eaves in summer, she would hear him return quite late at night, his voice loud and he would be laughing and singing until her mother shushed him. At a young age Teresa liked to hear her father happy at these times, but knew that inevitably the next day he would be sick again and have to stay all day in bed. On these mornings his daughters had to be extra quiet as they got on with their early morning chores.

Teresa had not like Herr Heinrich Mueller. He was fat and pompous, and always smelt funny as if he ate bad food. She hated it when he would bend down to her level, to pat her head or to kiss her cheek with his plump, fleshy lips. His mouth smelt really bad. Just like when the hens eggs, sometimes found under the hedgerows, after being hidden for weeks. As the town's mayor and police chief, he lived in a fine, large house with his equally fat wife and chubby son Gunter. Clara Mueller considering herself better than anyone and would often demand Hilde stitched, repaired or made her a garment immediately and for a small pittance. More than once when Frau Mueller was about to give a dinner party for her friends or Herr Mueller's influential cronies then it was her mother who they called upon to clean their house in readiness. Since those days, and as she got wiser to the ways of men and women, Teresa decided Frau Mueller was jealous of the way her husband looked longingly at the still beautiful woman. And even at such a young age Teresa didn't like the

21

way he came to their chalet driving his noisy, fume-belching black car, and the way the fat man would barge into their home without being invited. He had a way of looking at her mother in a funny way. She couldn't have put it into words but he made Teresa feel scared and uncertain, and it made her cross inside that he ordered Leisl and herself to play outside, because he wanted to talk to Hilde.

Why didn't *Mutti* stop him? Instead she would slowly nod her head towards her daughters as if agreeing.

And it hadn't stopped there, he would blatantly and without offering to pay, help himself to sacks of their freshly dug vegetables or the basket of eggs or mother's freshly baked bread from the oven, as if he had every right. None of this made sense to the seven year old Teresa, especially when she sensed her mother hadn't liked it either, when he put his arm around her shoulders and whispered something in her ear so quietly Teresa couldn't hear. Her mother's face would turn crimson, she would shrug him off and move away, only her face revealed true disgust and loathing. Never offended by her recoil, Mueller would laugh and snatch an apple from the dish on the table.

'He owns our farm and land so we must pay him rent and do what he wants. But promise me Teresa. No one must not know he's been here. It doesn't matter about the food, I will dig up more vegetables and make more bread. Herr Mueller helps us because your dear father needs expensive medicines and he can get these for me. So I --- we have to be nice to him. Your father mustn't know, but this is our little secret. Sometimes child, our Lord Jesus wants us to keep secrets from the people we love, because the truth would hurt them and we love your father very much. Do you understand *mien leibchen*?'

Teresa nodded obediently. Her mother often called upon the Good Lord Jesus and she also wanted to assure Him she could do her mother's bidding.

But no secrets were as dangerous as the ones yet to come.

Teresa had been only three when the village talked of the Anscluss, the annex of Austria by German in the spring of 1938. She didn't remember the excitement that was the talk of the village. March 12th her father, still hale and hearty in those days, had walked to the Heurigen and there had been and drinking and merriment throughout that night. Of course she'd not understood the significance of that day or what it meant. Nowadays the sight of the soldiers from the nearby garrison was a familiar sight, marching and strutting around their town. As she grew older her mother told her she must always be polite to the soldiers and salute, as she'd been shown, whenever they passed by. Above all try and keep out of their way as much as possible, they were important to their town and the country of Austria. It was *Vater* who spoke of the Germans and the Nazis, and something called The Greater German Reich. It all sounded mystifying and grand, and not fully understanding any of it, Teresa and the other children would often follow the smart lines of men in their grey uniforms, tin hats holding their rifles. They would chase after the columns of soldiers, laughing and mimicking their Fascist struts along the main street of their small rural town. She recognized one or two of the soldiers as some of the young men of the town had been proudly drafted into the German Wehrmacht. Their very important commandant, Oberfrüher Claus Schmit was a regular visitor at the big Mueller house across from the *Rathaus*. Heinrich Mueller liked to think of himself as a member of the SS Waffen although officially he wasn't regarded as part of the elite military unit, everyone seemed very impressed and in awe with this figure of authority and the town's people treated him with courtesy and reverence but many also an underlying distrust and fear.

In the rural towns and the cities of Austria a certain amount of propaganda had circulated amongst the population regarding the widespread Jewish communities. People muttered together, behind hands in small groups, of anti-Semitic intimidation and mob violence. It was only gossip, of course. Instigated by the brave and the stupid, but there were rumours that whole Jewish families were taken away in the dead of night, for their own safety. To be transported, packed into cattle trains and taken to special camps in places such as Dachau in Germany, or the newly built camp Mauthausen in north of Austria, built alongside the River Danube.

When there had been the unclarified news of the Kristallnacht (Night of Broken Glass) back in November 1938 and the discriminate burning of synagogues in Vienna, Josef Góetschl had always insisted this was scaremongering by the enemies of the State. After all hadn't he heard this from the mayor, who was so close to the army in power. It had to be the real truth.

Chapter 2

Teresa had been sad the morning in the spring of 1942, when she arrived at the school room for lessons and found it locked. She had been so looking forward to Herr Grassinger telling more about the ancient ruins of Carpathia. It had filled her mind with unimaginable wonders of a long lost civilization and its people, and quite unlike anything she knew. But the school was closed and it would remain so until Fraülein Weisz arrived some two months later. Teresa never fully understood why Herr Grassinger and his elderly mother had been taken away in the middle of the night to 'a place of safety'. He was nice, kind man and his mother was very old, why was it they were in such terrible danger they had to go somewhere secret? Teresa wanted to know the answers, but V*ater* was sick again with the seizures and must not be disturbed.

That morning she'd had the chance to ask Gunter, the twelve year old son of Clara and Heinrich Mueller. If anyone knew the answer to the puzzle, the son of the most important person in the town, would know it.

In the corner of the empty school playground she asked the bigger, heavily-built bully. He'd pinched Liesl's arm and demanded she let him pull her knickers down.

Leisl's eyes were red from crying and her nose ran onto the front of her new smock. Her arm was bruised and painful. Teresa pushed him hard, but he hardly moved, his small eyes mocked them both.

Teresa had screamed at him. 'Leave my sister alone.' She wasn't scared of him.

He'd then turned his cruel attention to the older sister, tugging at her long plaits until her head was really sore, and she was sure he would pull them from her head.

'Stop it, Gunter. You're hurting me.' She'd squirmed, but he'd only laughed and, twisting her plaits in his hands for more leverage, pulled harder.

With her little sister sobbing at her side, and just when she thought her hair would come away in his plump hands, she'd retaliated. It was all she could think of to taunt him with.

'I bet you don't know why Herr Grassinger has been taken away? You don't know anything,' she'd shouted, fighting back the tears of pain that sprang to her eyes and ran down her cheeks.

He'd let go and pushing his face into hers, sneered back at her in that superior 'know-it-all' way he'd had.

'That's easy. The teacher and his mother are 'undesirables' and are not allowed to live here anymore.'

It was Teresa turn to be confused.

'What are undesirables? What does that mean?' she'd asked, momentarily forgetting the sore patch on her head, finally getting free of his plump, grasping fists and taking the crying Leisl's hand they'd moved to a safer distance.

'My father,' he'd stuck out his chest in pride, 'the mayor and police chief says it is part of The Final Solution. I don't expect you, just a stupid, ignorant girl to understand, but The Greater German Reich must be cleansed of all --- 'undesirables.''

He'd ended the statement as if uncertain himself. It was a speech that, had Teresa been older and more knowledgeable, would surely have been recognized as being repeated word for word from something told by his father. But Teresa didn't understand. His explanation made no sense, but she would ask her father when he was feeling better. Teresa never did get an answer to her questions, not

26

until years later, and Albert Grassinger and his mother were never seen in the town again.

There were whispers behind closed door, but these ceased after the garrison commandant, the Oberführuer moved into the Grassinger's house seizing the leather bound books, oil paintings, antique furniture and any valuables that were left behind.

Fraülein Weisz, brought reluctantly from her home in Salzburg to take over as temporary teacher, was obviously furious at this new posting and made sure her pupils suffered. In her fifties she was very tall and very thin, and her face was fierce and unfriendly. A strict disciplinarian she ruled the class with a stick that often came down loudly on the edge of her desk to make a point, or more often on a pupil's knuckles. Teresa didn't like her one bit, and especially when she seemed to take a particular dislike to her friend who sat next to her in class, nine year old Stefan Reiter.

It seemed Stefan could do no right in the woman's eyes. He was small for his age. He lived at the edge of the town quite close to the Göetschls, with his widowed mother and six siblings. As the only boy had to help her run their smallholding on his own, it wasn't surprising he often fell asleep during the fraülein's long jingoistic monologues. His worn, patched clothes, his determined attitude not to be beaten by her humiliation, meant he came in for her punishment more than any other student.

Fraülein Weisz had little time for books or the classics, but apart from a few hours of basic reading, writing and arithmetic, preferred to spend the school hours instilling in her class the terrible atrocities done by the Allies against the *wunderbar* German people and how Adolf Hitler would rain terror down on these evil nations and the Reich would live forever. Her scowling face would soften and she'd stare over the heads of the class to the large colored poster of Mein Führer pinned on the far wall, and her eyes would take on a strange, fanatic expression.

It meant nothing to Teresa, and the rest of the class, having to stand to military attention at their desks four times every day giving the familiar Fascist salute and singing patriotic songs, or the endless stiff and 'marching in strict time' around the school playground. She missed the stories Herr Grassinger would often read from one of his colourful spine books on the shelf behind him. Those books of marvel were gone now to be replaced by booklets and leaflets of Anti-Semitism and Nazi Power.

There was an atmosphere of doubt and mistrust that even someone as young as Teresa sensed and of course, there were more strange disappearance in the town that no one liked to talk about.

'But *Mutti,* why have the Herr and Frau Winkler left their pawnbroker's shop and where have they gone?'

Her mother was always afraid when Teresa asked these bold questions: checking no one had overheard her eager daughter's query, especially at the crowded stall on market day. Close by two soldiers were talking and smoking and one glanced in their direction.

'Shush Teresa,' she hissed as the purchases were placed in her basket and she handed over the coins. 'They have gone away. I think they are staying with their daughter and her family in the Tauern Valley.'

'They are having a holiday? When are they coming back, *Mutti*?'

The Winkler's nine year old daughter Rachel sat in the desk behind Teresa. Sometimes they would giggle together during classes and often get into trouble with Fraülein Weisz.

'I don't know, now shush child. Go and collect Leisl she's at the toymaker's stall. We must hurry home to get *Vatti* his lunch.'

But the Winkler's never came back from holiday and soon Teresa forgot to ask her mother when Rachel would be returning. Fraülein Weisz moved Gunter to the desk immediately behind Teresa's and she had to suffer his constant pulling and tugging of her plaits, knowing that if she complained or cried out she would be the one who'd be punished. That changed when she persuaded her mother to pin her plaits around her head. Not one to be deterred the Mueller boy soon found he could annoy her more, by kicking at her legs under the desk.

Even worse was when her friend Stefan Reiter didn't turn up to school one day in June. It seemed that overnight Frau Reiter, Stefan and his five sisters had left their rundown small-holding and gone away, and without telling anyone. Her father having spent the day in the Heurigen heard the news from the butcher, who was definitely talking louder than was wise after one glass of wine too many, that as they were Gypsies it was no surprise they'd been arrested and taken to a camp. Their small-holding now abandoned and forgotten, soon became no more than an overgrown ramshackle ruin. Like the Winkler family before them, Teresa with an understanding beyond her years, realized that there were certain things that were not to be discussed in front of others, or her father.

There had always been a framed picture of Our Lord pinned on the wall above the pine dresser. Beside it on a hook was Hilde's rosary and crucifix. Every day she would cross herself and kiss the small, gold cross on getting up and before she went to bed. In the top drawer of the dresser there were more rosaries. One for Teresa and Leisl, the one that was Josef's although he never took it out, not even on Sunday's or even saints' days. There was a well-worn one, the cross ornately enamelled in jewel-like colors that had belonged to her grandmother, and amongst the others a broken rosary that had shed its hard, black beads amongst the general detritus accumulated at the bottom.

It was the only time she ever heard her father make her mother cry, when one day on his return from the

Heurigen and having spent his time amongst a handful of German soldiers, he had brought back with him a photograph of the same strange-looking, sinister man that now hung on the back wall of the school room. Her mother cried hard and long but knew it was useless to object when the picture of Our Lord was taken down and Hitler's photo pinned there in its place.

Teresa didn't like his face. He had small, piercing eyes beneath a black lick of hair, and a silly little moustache beneath his beaky nose that looked more like one of the hairy caterpillars that ate *Mutti's* cabbage leaves. She'd pointed a small finger at the picture and giggled at the image. She'd thought he looked very silly and told her father so, as she doubled up with uncontrollable childish mirth.

Josef was furious with his daughter. That day he'd had the strength to slap her face hard, twice, shouting at her to get out of his sight.

He had never hit his children before and it had shocked not just Teresa but his wife. Her father had always been so gentle and patient, and she ran crying, hurt and confused, to her mother. Hilde, secretly disturbed by this unexpected and 'out of character' incident, comforted her sobbing daughter, but made her promise never to speak ill of the man in the photo again. The mark of his fingerprints on Teresa's cheeks soon faded, but not the pain of his outburst, deep in her heart. But she never broke her promise either, even when Josef decided that instead of genuflecting each morning and night, the family should all give the Führer, Nazi salutes.

'This is not a subject for the confessional Teresa,' her mother told her in a quiet moment. 'It must not get back to Father Dominic's ears.'

Teresa had shrugged her shoulders and solemnly nodded. She didn't understand what was happening in their lovely town anymore. So much had changed since the German soldiers set up the garrison a few kilometers away, and Oberfrüher Schmit moved into the former teacher's house. It seemed to ask questions only brought more confusion and pain.

The young priest Father Dominic she was sure would have understood, and maybe he could have answered the hundreds of questions that always seemed to be filling her head. He was vague but nice and patted the children's heads during Sunday school. He rarely smiled, as if to be solemn and serious was best for his 'calling', but when he smiled his face reminded her of the picture of Our Lord that now resided in the drawer in the dresser beneath the broken rosary beads. He must be kind and loving just like Jesus, but even so she heeded her mother and kept quiet.

It was a hot, clear day in late August the sky a deep blue with wisps of clouds, touching the tips of the mountains in the distance. The fresh air smelt of wild flowers and honey, and behind the chalet the clear water rippled and sang over the pebbles in the stream. The girls feasted on the sweet wild strawberries that grew on the hillside, and picked as many as would fill their baskets.

Josef was sick. He'd had two seizures in quick succession and lay inside on the couch, the windows and door wide open. He could hear the nanny goats on the side of the hill and the hens busily clucking and scratching in the dirt under the hedges. If he turned his head, he could just see through the window the tops of the thick pine trees that skirted the nearest hill, backing onto the misty outlines and the rise of further hills in the distance. He never tired of looking at that scene. Somewhere close by he could hear his daughters playing and chasing the geese that grumbled and cackled at such undignified treatment.

From his position on the couch he was able to peer across the room to the photograph. He had long since dismissed the distress that its presence had first caused. Here he imagined he saw in the face, strength and resolute, the firm jaw lines and eyes of fiery determination. Herr Hitler,

31

also an Austrian, would save and unite the two most important countries in the world. Josef Gőetschl believed passionately the propaganda and speeches he'd listened to almost daily from the groups of influential Nazis that gathered in the Heurigen. Never once doubting the truth or sincerity repeated time and again by the fanatical Henrich Mueller and equally fanatic Claus Schmit both knew so much of the world than he. With a sigh of deep satisfaction that irritated the delicate membranes in his chest and bringing a bout of coughing, he rested his head back against the cushion and closed his eyes. Hilde would be back from the town soon and she already had the ingredients prepared for a tasty evening meal. Maybe food would sustain him enough for another evening in the wine hall spent in the interesting company of his Nazi friends.

To Teresa and the rest of the children in the town, the soldiers in the nearby garrison was no more intimidating or frightening than the men, in their official looking uniforms, that actually policed the town.

One warm, afternoon after school, they were in the town's central square. It was a cobbled area large enough for market days, with solid, stone slab benches placed outside the townhall and the imposing clock tower, atop the old building, chimed out the hours with regularity and precision.

A young soldier lounging against the wall, chatting and smoking with his friends, broke away from the others and sauntered towards the bench where Teresa, her friend Ingrid and Leisl sat. Teresa thought he was about the same age as Bernard Fischer, the eighteen year old son of the miller, but were as Bernard was loud and boisterous, this soldier was very serious, with a strange fierce light in his eyes. He was made to look older than his years by the oversized heavy, dark uniform, the tin hat that sat low on his brow and the rifle, they all carried one, slung of one shoulder. The tall, blonde boy with eyelashes so fair as to be invisible in the strong, afternoon sun strolled up to the girls and after moving the rifle so he held it loosely in his hand, he placed a jack-booted foot on the stone beside Ingrid. He was hot in the uniform and with his free hand took off his helmet to wipe his forehead dripping with beads of sweat. He gazed down at the three, who gazed back in puzzlement unsure what to think they looked from his face to their friends at their side. As if by an unspoken understanding the majority of the foot soldiers patrolled the town and the surrounding areas with little interest in its inhabitants, but he seemed friendly enough and he lifted his serious, with the almost colourless eyes, so he could feel the sun on his skin. He half closed his eyes savouring this rare moment of relaxation.

'My name's Franz,' he told them with the recognizable accent change of the German speaking Deutch.' I'm from Berlin. I have three younger sisters like you.'

He paused again to wipe his face on his tunic sleeve. 'It is very hot today. In Germany, before the war, when it was too hot all my family, aunts, uncles, cousins and grandparents, we would go to the countryside where it was cooler, fresher. Not anymore. Not since the English killed most of them with their bombing raids in 1940. Only my mother and my sisters were saved.'

He put his foot back on the ground, returned his helmet to his head so effectively they couldn't see his eyes and clasped his rifle with both hands taking up an aggressive stance.

'But the Luftwaffe blitzkrieg London and many die,' he said in a clipped decisive manner heavy with obvious delight.

The three girls didn't understand. Teresa didn't know what blitzkrieg meant, and wonder why it made this man so happy that so many people in London died. London was the capital of England. She knew this because their old teacher Herr Grassinger had told them and shown them on his globe were England was and told them all about its people. Teresa had thought it sounded a nice place to live.

Now Franz from Berlin was happy to kill these people.

As if reading her confused thoughts the young soldier pulled the rifle back on his shoulder.

'Do not feel sorry for them,' he insisted watching their expressions. 'They are an evil people, always killing. Kill, kill, kill. Kill everyone, women and children and little babies. But do not be frightened, our great Führer for the good of the fatherland, will defeat them all. He will be victorious.'

He suddenly gave the salute with his arm raised high, lifted his chin in defiance and goose-stepped back to join his comrades leaning against a wall. They were chatting and smoking, and with cheers and cat-calls, boisterously encouraged and applauded his sentiment.

Teresa often saw Franz in the town or marching in step on patrol, and although her insatiable thirst to learn: her mind full of questions about just about anything, bombings, blitzkrieg, the War, she never got a chance to ask the young soldier more.

Chapter 3

'Oh there you are, Frau Gőetschl.'

It was a cold early autumn Friday and the town's market place was awash with brightly colored stalls. Mother and daughters had been out early, especially to buy sewing needles, threads and material from the haberdashery, and to the fish stall for the family's evening meal.

Clara Mueller was running to catch up with them as they walked quickly away from the market place in the direction of home.

With Leisl clutching her mother's hand and Teresa skipping at her side swinging the basket of shopping she sensed her mother tense. They stopped to let the fat woman catch up. Frau Mueller was breathing hard, her plump cheeks red with unfamiliar exertion.

'Just the person I've been looking for,' she wheezed clutching her fleshy hand to her enormous bosom. 'I have a very important job for you. I repeat it is of paramount importance. Whatever else you're sewing or stitching at the moment, I must insist you put it to one side ---.'

Hilde was about to say that she wanted to get her daughters thick woollen coats completed before the really cold weather set in, but was stopped from saying anything with the mayor's wife raising her hand to silence any objections or contradictions.

'I repeat! I insist, and not just me, but my husband and the commandant Oberführer Claus Schmit. It has been decided that every child in the town must wear an arm band displaying the glorious swastika. It is the duty of all good Austrian's, and you have been appointed to make these armbands. They are all to be the same and must take priority over anything else.'

Her face was beaming with delight and her eyes shown with the light of fanaticism, although Teresa wouldn't know it as that, but right that moment the young girl saw only a fat, older woman who suddenly gripped her mother's arm, squeezing it hard until Hilde winced.

'You won't let the Party down, now will you dear Frau Gőetschl?' It was said with a hint of a threat. And of course Teresa's mother agreed to this unusual demand.

Teresa remembered clearly, just how long it had taken her mother to complete this mammoth order. She had stitched and sewn the countless armbands, often from dawn to dusk, until her fingers were sore, from holding the fine needles, her eyes bloodshot with the strain and her head ached through sheer exhaustion. There seemed to be hundreds, all the same, dull grey flannel with the prominent oddly-shaped black cross. Josef often sat and watched his quiet wife at her work, he was proud of her and commented often on the magnificent task she was undertaking for the Party. Hilde stayed silent: she had no need to give her opinion, only wishing in her heart that she was stitching the finally seams on the coats for her daughters, and wondering if she'd ever get paid for all the work.

Eventually the job was done and Heinrich Mueller congratulated her on such fine needlework, unfortunately no payment was offered and her husband thought it would be insulting to ask for any. The armbands were to be handed out to the people in a civil ceremony in front of the townhall. Mueller had decided it was of such importance, cementing the alliance between the Germans and this small Austrian town, that not only was Oberfrüher Schmit to be the guest of honour but the town's band had to rehearse and rehearse the German national anthem until they had every note perfect, so they could play it on the day.

36

Of course, along with other children, Leisl and Teresa had been made to wear them every day: at home, school or in the town. At first they felt strange on the upper arm, each held tight with strips of elastic, over bulky garments. But this was something they had to get use to. Gradually over the weeks and months the slipping on the armbands, every morning, became as natural as combing and plaiting their long hair.

It was the autumn of 1942 and by November it had turned very cold. This year it seemed winter had arrive even earlier in their valley beneath the hills and distant mountains.

'Teresa, *mein leibchen,*' Josef had said one morning. 'After school I want you go and bring the goats down from the hills. It is time to put them in their home for the winter. Make sure they have plenty of feed.'

It was her job to look after the nanny goats and their kids, to feed them and milk them and as a treat she could have the warm, sweet milk fresh from the swollen teats. She remembered it always tasted so good and, she would make sure to fill a mug and take it to Leisl waiting inside the chalet.

That evening she buttoned up her new woollen coat made by her mother, and wrapped a long scarf around her head then pulled on her mittens. Outside the ends of her fingers soon tingled with the first bite of the winter's frost.

'Now make sure you hurry the silly animals into the falling-down barn before it gets dark,' her mother had insisted, carefully stirring the big pan of bubbling rabbit and root vegetables on the stove. The large room filled with the inviting, appetizing smell. It made Teresa's mouth water as she'd she slipped out through the door and into the chilled air that caught at her throat. She shivered and pulled the scarf up around her mouth and nose, and her knitted hat down low, so there was hardly any of her face exposed to the cold. She quickly skirted the first hill then ran up the small incline towards their animals: perched on a narrow stony ridge they were sheltered from the worst of the wind. It took little encouragement for them to follow the girl down and into the barn. They would be there most of the coming winter except for bright days when they could be tethered in the yard.

'*Mutti* calls you silly animals,' she admonished one as the nanny tried to butt her away. 'And I think she is right, you silly Gertrude.'

But with the experience of having done this chore many times she sidestepped the elderly nanny, and turned her attention to their feed. It was an early dusk outside and the wind, picking up in strength, moaned and whistled through the gaps in the walls wooden planks, rattled the warped window frame at the side, and the loose fitting doors front and rear. Overhead through the a hole at one side Teresa could just make out the darkening sky the colour of ochre with the low-lying clouds sweeping towards the town from their previous residence on top of the mountains. These were the foretaste of an approaching snow storm. Teresa knew the signs: by morning the entire landscape, stretching as far as the eye could see, across the hills, the valley basins and balanced on the tops of the trees would have changed dramatically to one of a white winter wonderland.

The goats quickly settled to accommodate their own space, but equally used to sharing their winter home with the scattering of clucking hens roosting along the sills and up amongst the hay in the overhead loft.

Teresa stared nervously up at the shadows in the low-ceiling loft. She always thought that with the sound of the wind whistling eerily overhead, the hay loft was quite scary. Of course there was always the possibility of there being mice or worse, rats overhead. She hated rats. Had she heard them now? Was the slight shuffling and scurrying sound the proof that there were families of rodents in their falling-down barn?

Teresa wasn't about to find out for herself by staying any longer than she needed. Running outside she hurriedly slammed shut the double doors and fixed the padlock in place, just in case Herr Fox was on the prowl then ran back to the warm, cozy house and the meal waiting for her.

Inside the barn the goats moved and shifted around, disturbing the chickens with collective unease. Something wasn't right, something felt out of place from their familiar surroundings. Gertrude and her family reared and butted the fetid air, their nostrils flared with growing unease.

In the loft the man and woman, and small boy, moved closer to help conserve their body heat. Below, once the girl had shut and bolted the door, they knew they had no way of escape, but would have to stay until the morning. What the daylight held they preferred not to consider. It was almost too cold to worry about their fate, when the next few hours stretched before them. It was so cold. The boy moaned and thrashed in his mother's arms. He was running a fever and she was sick with worry, and concern for her sick child. The man, taking a tin mug from a small bag, their only possession they now had left, he cautiously climbed down the rickety ladder. There he nervously approached one of the nanny goats, her udders held the sustenance for his child. He'd never milked a cow or a goat before: he never in his thirty years been near a farm, but this was not the time to baulk at this life sustaining task.

The next day the snow covered the ground in a continuous unspoilt carpet. After school, holding Leisl's hand firmly, the sister's ran and skipped back home. The layer of snow was firm underfoot, crisp and crunching with a pleasurable sound beneath their boots. They pursed their mouth into 'O' shapes, so their breath came as long wisps in the freezing, but crisp air. Their breath looked just like the blue smoke from their father's mouth when he smoked one of his cigarettes. The pretended they had cigarettes between their fingers and could copy the *Vater*.

The girls had their usual chores before they could eat, and before they did their set homework. Fraulein Weisz always set her pupils homework in relation to the life of Hitler, and this day was no different.

But first, logs needed bringing in to feed the fire for the night ahead. The animals in the falling-down barn needed feeding. Icicles hook like long, daggers from the roof and in the semi-light the ground seemed to sparkled and dance with millions of gemstones. There was going to be a bad storm already building and ready to sweep down from the mountains, with a cruel, relentless ferocity.

The smell of the bread, just out of the oven and the mouthwatering soup packed full of carrots, turnips, onions and rich herb dumplings meant they would hurry through their chores extra quickly.

'Teresa, your father has had a bad day again, so I've not had the chance to collect the eggs.' Teresa took the egg basket, from the shelf and the two stepped outside.

Leisl loaded her small arms with the logs, stacked against the outer wall, and ran back inside.

Teresa hurried across the solid, frozen ground to the barn doors. The first dainty snowflakes were falling meaning she left her footprints in the fine layer. The wind was gathering strength and almost knocked the young girl off her feet as she tugged at the padlock and pulled back one of the double doors.

The goats gathered around her expectantly. Teresa spoke to them as they pushed and nudged against her legs.

'Gertrude, Matilda stop that.'

The hens clucked and pecked around her feet. First she checked the different places for eggs.

Just five. In all the usual places, in the corners amongst drifts of grimy straw that had scattered across the earth ground.

She would check if the little white hen, Leisl had called Giselle had laid a second. Not today.

Inside the barn, the wind again moaned through the cracks and crevices. Draught, from the hole in the roof, suddenly sent a scattering of straw from the hayloft to the uneven ground below, covering Teresa. She scowled and brushed it off the sleeve of her coat, then checked everything. The animals had food and water, the eggs were in the basket. Inside the house, her own warming meal beckoned.

She pushed open the door once more, struggling against the sudden force

Of the wind and was about to step outside into the fast falling snow. In just a matter of minutes it had already formed low drifts against the walls of the barn and she could make out the covering across the steep slope of the chalet's roof.

She paused. She was certain she'd heard something behind her. Not the sounds of the animals but something else.

With her heart beating fast and her hand on the door catch, Teresa stopped and listened. Was it one of the young goats? Had one of the kids made a strange bleating sound?

No, this was someone crying. A child? The crying, at first muffled, was getting louder and more pitiful then abruptly the sound stopped. Overhead a sudden gust of wind rattled a loose slate on the ancient roof making her jump.

Had she imagined the crying? Feeling a little brave, even if her body wouldn't stop shaking, she pulled the door open one more and stepped over the threshold into the old, falling-down barn. One of the hens, eager for more grain pecked the ground around her boots. One extra careful footstep after the other, Teresa, tiptoed to the foot of the ladder leading to the dark, shadowy loft. A movement, a small scuffling sound, a shadow across a beam and she gasped, a hand flying to her mouth. These weren't rodents in the loft.

Then the sound: the crying started again and this time the sound was pitiful. This time, over the sobs Teresa heard a desperate, whispered voice. A woman's voice.

The old woman eased her shoe back on and lifted her head. In the distance the town hall clock told her it was half past twelve and time to be getting back. Ms Riley would be getting impatient for her shopping and in any case her remembered thoughts of Mutti's lovely rich warming stew that had been waiting for her on finishing her chores was suddenly making her hungry. It was coming back to her like figures hidden in a fog. The man, woman and child she'd discovered hiding in the loft.

Nervously but with heightened confidence, knowing it wasn't after all the big, fat rats making nests amongst the straw, she climbed the steps. She sensed she should have run back to her parents and told them, but she wanted to see for herself.

They sat together in a huddle in the corner of the loft. A man and woman, about the same age as her own parents, were crouched amongst the straw. Between them was a small boy of about four or five. Teresa stared and they stared back with alarm and trepidation.

'Who are you?' she hardly dared speak and they looked to be as horrified as the girl now standing firm in front of them. The last of the light revealed the white faces streaked with grime, their clothes caked in mud. The boy whimpered and his mother stroked his forehead and pulled him closer to her.

Teresa was reminded of the gypsies her father had warned her to avoid and telling her. 'Remember Teresa, gypsies can snatch young girl's from their families, so I you must never to talk to them.'

He had issued this dire warning after her friend Stefan Reiter and the Reiter family had been proclaimed to be dirty gypsies and just simply disappeared. Secretly Teresa had not thought the slight, dark skinned, curly headed boy dirty, nor his mother and sisters. The few times she'd visited their smallholding when they still lived there, the place, although a little rundown was always spotlessly clean. Not that she mentioned this fact to her father, instinctively knowing to keep her own council.

Now the very people her father had warned her about, unkempt and obviously dirty, where here hiding in their falling-down barn. Would they snatch her and take her away to their camp, just as *Vater* had said, and before she could call for help?

She was alarmed when the man stood and moved closer so he was standing so close he could have reached out and grabbed her.

'Little girl,' he said low and in a strange accent she didn't recognize.

That was all Teresa needed, she ran to the ladder and almost fell down in her haste to get away. She didn't look back to see if he'd followed her but ran to the door and heaved it shut, grateful to hear the wood slam against the jamb. Never mind fixing the padlock in place, she wanted to get home to safety.

What of the goats, Gertrude and Matilda and the kids, and the hens, would these gypsies leave them alone?. Who knew what they would do to the animals if they had been unable to 'snatch' her, She was so frightened she couldn't breathe and she gasped and stumbled across the uneven fine layer of fallen snow, back towards the chalet with its light shining invitingly and the safety of her family inside.

'*Mutti. Mutti. Vater,*' Teresa yelled at the top of her lungs as she ran as fast as she could along the worn path from the barn to the house. She was out of breath when she pushed open the door and almost fell inside: sudden rush of heat from the banked up fire hitting her cold cheeks with the force of a wall.

With her hand on her chest to check her racing heart she leaned against the inside of the door and then it was she noticed Leisl was in her preferred place under the large pine table cuddling her doll and sucking her thumb with the look of fear on her face. That could mean only one thing her father was having another bad turn. Josef lay prone on the floor, the foam still oozing from his pale mouth, his eyes half closed in exhaustion, his pallor the colour of sour milk. At his feet the hand woven rag rug was rucked up into a ball where his heels had drummed and shuffled as his tense body fought against the spasms.

'Shush. Teresa. *Vatti* is poorly. Help me get him into bed and then you must eat your meal and get you and your sister ready for bed.'

Teresa didn't need telling twice. This had been her role so many times before the seven year old got on with doing her mother's bidding and for the moment the gypsies in the hayloft were forgotten.

By the morning, Josef was feeling better and instead of staying in bed at the insistence of his wife, he stood on the threshold smoking a calming cigarette and breathing in the clear mountain air. The overnight flurry of snow had settled into a thick layer covering the uneven ground surrounding the chalet, but was quickly melting with the surprising warmth from the sun shining from a blue sky that stretched far towards the fluffy cloud-topped mountains to the north towards the distant grey, misty mountains to the west across the border into Switzerland. A bird sang happily in one of the tall trees growing behind the low wooden building while the goats released from the confines of the barn skittered and skipped, nudging at Teresa and Leisl for more food held in the folds of their pinafores, and the hens scratched and clucked at the ground searching for grubs or the grains of feed they might have missed previously. Once her daughters had eaten their breakfast and she'd made sure

Josef was settled, they would be heading along the well walked path, over the hill to the church for early morning Mass, then leaving the girls to make their way to the schoolroom she would head home to start on the repairs on a blouse for the butcher's wife.

Hilde, an attractive woman in her early thirties never forgot to thank Jesus for her life, her lovely daughters and her good fortune in being married to her man and praying with all her heart that one day he would be well again. She never doubted His compassion.

She thought again of the medicine she'd been able to get from Heinrich Mueller thanks to his contact with the German commandant. Only this medicine could help her beloved Josef and she would always do whatever it took to ensure she never ran out of the pills.

Later, she walked slowly back home savoring the gentle, cooling breeze on her face and the way it tugged playfully at the skein of hair plaited and wrapped around her head. She pulled her coat around her as the chill reminded her it was November and from the signs of clouds gathering over the mountains the snow of the previous night was only the beginning of winter. With the knowledge of someone born and bred in the Tyrol she knew that tonight would be even colder than the last.

Hilde was not altogether surprised to find Josef was not at home when she got back. He would take every opportunity to make the most of the good weather and will have taken his usual stroll, not to overdo it, to the Heurigen in the town in the valley. He deserved his small pleasures, like a chance to meet with his friends and have a flagon or two, after all he was an invalid who suffered his infirmities daily.

Something, a sound different to what she'd expected and the fact the barn door had been left open, made her stop in front of the barn. Teresa knew better than to leave the door open after collecting the eggs, there was always the risk of foxes or vermin sneaking in and attacking the animals once shut away for the night.

'Gertrude,' she remonstrated with the large nanny goat as she head butted the woman. 'What was the girl thinking to leave this open? Get away from me you silly beast.'

She shut the door with a final flourish and marched with growing irritation to the door of the chalet. It was unlatched. Not Josef too? But she was growing alarmed. Her family, Teresa, Leisl and Josef were reliable, why would any one of them leave doors open like this?

Perhaps Josef wasn't at the Heurigen after all --. Maybe ---. Oh no. ---A thought made her gasp in fright. What if her husband had had another seizure and had only managed to get inside before he collapsed? What would she find when she stepped into her large, warm home?

Chapter 4

She held her breath for a second or two, stepped inside and only then called out, 'Josef.'

The first thing she noticed was the low whimpering of a child. Was it one of her daughters?

'Teresa. Leisl.' She didn't wonder why her girls might be back, only there was something wrong.

In the semi light from the small window and the sunlight streaming in from the open door behind her Hilde's eyes took a moment to adjust to the interior.

She gazed in amazement at the strangers. They were circling the fire hands outstretched towards the heat. The man turned at the sound of Hilde's voice and he was visibly shaking. The woman pulled the small boy into the folds of her skirt and seemed to sway, about to fall down.

They appeared to be dressed in good clothing. The coat worn by the woman looked of good quality, as did the man's jacket and trousers. Their shoes, although dirty and muddy looked to be made from the finest leather. The boy, possibly around three years of age in woollen trousers and coat was wrapped in the traditional weaved cover that had been left, neatly folded, on the top of the settle used as a bed during the winter by her girls. All this her mind took in, in a matter of seconds, but they were here inside her home to rob her or worse and she was sudden afraid. She knew they had nothing of value, so what could they want?

Yet there was something about this pathetic family group that overtook any sense of a threat. A mixture of relief and pity took over as she stared back at this obviously frightened group. The man ran a nervous tongue around his thin, pinched lips and for the second time his eyes turned to the photograph of Hitler on the Góetschl's wall. There was stark fear in the depths of his dark, almost black, eyes.

'What are you doing in my home?' Hilde asked in a whisper, almost afraid that by disturbing the silence and perfectly still tableau before her, she would be in danger.

'What do you want?' Hilde hesitated, her words sticking in her dry throat.

'You see. We have nothing---,' she said swinging her arm wide as if confirming her statement.

The boy, with eyes the colour of jet, peered out from his mother's skirt. He coughed a deep hacking cough that seemed to envelope his small, thin body.

They were a threat, just cold frightened and lost. Making up her mind she closed the door, shutting out the chill wind. Without really thinking what she was doing, Hilde crossed to a shelf, picked up a bottle and poured a measure of the warming honey and spice mixture into a tiny cup. They stood and watched her movements without a sound. Only the child convulsed with coughing, whimpered pitifully.

Hilde passed the mixture to the mother. She smiled gratefully, one mother to another.

'Please sit,' said Hilde and watched, as once seated on the settle with the boy on her knew, the woman coaxed her son to drink. His coughing gradually eased and he seemed calmer.

For the first time the woman spoke. 'Thank you. *Herzlichen dank*, Frau.'

The man watching, still standing swayed slightly.

'Sit. Please sit,' invited Hilde and he took the space at the side of his wife.

Hilde, her initial fear long forgotten, felt only sympathy for these people who had invaded her home, but still she unconsciously fingered the crucifix hanging from her neck, as if it reassured her.

It seemed that the man and the woman visibly relaxed. The man rested against the back and momentarily closed his eyes. Hilde guessed the couple was around her age, but with the recently formed lines of worry across their brows, the pale almost grey pallor of fear and hunger, and the way their shoulders hunched against the possible terrors, they could have been much older.

The woman's only concern was her sick child and she held him against her chest gently rocking him, crooning low a tune Hilde hadn't heard before.

'We --- we are grateful for your help. We would not have come here but our son --- you understand?' The man opened his eyes and again his gaze was drawn to the face peering down at them from the wall. He pulled his mesmerized gaze away from the terrifying image, and searched her face as if hoping to find compassion there.

'We are ---,' he began. He swallowed the words then his eyes strayed back to the photo as if its very malevolent presence made him uneasy. To heighten the sense of unease, his eyes flicked quickly to the door half expecting the man in the photo, or his troopers, to burst in.

'Never mind,' Hilde spoke with a sudden firm conviction. 'You can explain later, after you've had something to eat and drink. Pull the settle closer to the fire you are freezing.' Together they moved the seat closer and sat as Hilde busied herself with the pans on the range. She noticed, but didn't comment, on the steam and smell of damp wool that arose in the room. Without a sound they watched as she set about making hot drinks, cutting thick slabs of homemade bread, chunks of goat's cheese and filling dishes with hot, tasty soup. The man and woman watched her every move and then when beckoned, the child tight in the fold of the woman's arm, sat at the pine table and ate hungrily. The child stared at the food and it was good to see take a few pieces of the bread soaked in the soup before he rested his head back against his mother and closed his eyes. Hilde would have offered to hold the boy so the woman could eat her fill, but the wary look still strong in her eyes told her to leave it be. Slowly as they ate and drank, and some vestige of colour came to their sallow cheeks, the man spoke.

'My name is Szabó, Karl Szabó and this is my wife Esther and our son David. We have travelled a long way in many days.'

Hilde guessed this, but wisely didn't pry or ask question. Even here she knew better. She knew they were Hungarians, their accents and clothes told her that much. And she knew they were Jews. And this knowledge made her heart race and she tightened her hold on her crucifix and said a prayer to Jesus under her breath.

As if reading her thoughts the man continued.

'We will go. If you could just let my wife and our child have a short rest.'

The boy, David doubled up with a sudden new bout of coughing. The sound tore at Hilde's heart and the sound made her ponder all this for a few minutes. No matter the politics or the rights or wrongs, here was an innocent sick child. Her Lord had never turned away those sick or desperate, whoever they were and she wasn't about to turn this family out into the cold, whatever the possible outcome. She looked at Esther as she held her child, rubbed his back, smoothing a strand of fine hair off his forehead that was obviously damp with fever. Tentatively she coaxed him with a sip from the mug of warm fresh milk, but he pushed it away. He whimpered and choked as phlegm filled his throat.

'We have no right to ask this of you,' Esther said without raising her tired eyes, but sensing the kindred maternal feeling that passed unspoken between the two. 'We have been in the hay loft of your barn for two nights, and it was very cold, but the heat from the goats helped. If we could go back there for one more night at least, in the morning we will be gone.'

Hilde listened and was filled with dismay. Even with the small herd of goats giving off some heat from their warm coats, the barn was full of draughts and not water tight. Another night and she didn't hold out much hope for this little boy and what could quickly turn to fatal pneumonia if he didn't get some decent food and wasn't kept warm.

She closed her eyes and kept tight hold of the crucifix. What was she to do? Josef would instantly turn this young family over to his German friends. Hungarian Jews had been persecuted for years and the Szabó family didn't stand a chance if the likes of Heinrich Mueller got to hear of them.

But it wasn't just these refugees who would be in danger. Her own family, her daughters and possibly Josef would be arrested as enemies of the Greater German Reich transported to one of the labor camps, or worse, they could be shot.

What was she to do? Any moment her husband could return and find them here. In just a couple of hours Teresa and Leisl would be home from school. They must never know about these unexpected visitors. A word or sentence innocently said or spoken in haste to one of Teresa's friends, Ingrid or Greta, or said in anger to Gunter Mueller, and they could all end up disappearing like many had in the town.

No time to waste. Time had passed and already the early dusk and mist was settling like a cloak on the hills. The child coughed until his small body doubled in pain and already his cheeks inflamed with a critically rising temperature. They watched her without guile. It was perhaps very unwise, but the woman, at least, had to put her trust in this Austrian frau who had offered them food and warmth, and above all her boy must be safe.

As if reading her thoughts Hilde said, 'I don't know, or want to know where you've come from or where you are going. What I do know is your child would not survive another freezing night in the barn.'

She struggled to sort it out in her mind.

'My husband and my daughters will be home soon and I don't want them to find you here.'

How could she just turn them out into what was promising to be another freezing night, with a child so sick and in great danger from the surrounding army of Nazis? She simply couldn't get the story of the Good Samaritan out of her mind. Did the Lord want her to play the Good Samaritan now and give these poor people food and shelter? Maybe He was telling her to keep them safe and to help them as much as possible. She would pray extra hard and ask for guidance. Later. But right now ---.

Any moment her family would be coming home. The thought of Josef, with his new found beliefs and knowing he would straight away turn them over to Mueller and the camp commandant without a second's thought, meant she must act quickly. She would listen in silence to his long tirades of the good of the Third Reich, the propaganda and all the other ideology that her husband had embraced with so much vigour and fervor it seemed to damage his already failing health. But she had her own thoughts and kept them from Josef.

But right now what was she to do?

Already the thought of being found out even having these people, what Josef referred to as 'undesirables' in her house had caused patches of damp to form under her arms and along the ridge of her spine.

Think fast. Act now.

The uncertainty mixed with the light of raw fear was obvious on Hilde's face and the woman Esther spoke. She had looked closely at the other's changing expressions, reading the initial determination, to uncertainly and fright.

'We should go,' she rose clutching her child tightly. He moaned in a restless sleep. 'Thank you for the food and

52

warmth. You are most kind, but we cannot put you and your family in danger.'

Her husband stood and stretched out his arms towards his wife. His face was weary and his eyes filled with frustrated tears. Why was he unable to keep his family safe? Why had they to be hunted like animals just because of their faith? It didn't make sense.?

Hilde, as if getting the Devine message she was hoping for, as she listened to the wind picking up and the first flurry of snow beating against the window. Her prayers to the Lord God, Mother Mary and the Baby Jesus had never let her down.

'Quickly,' she rushed to the ladder propped against the wall that was the only means to the trap door leading to the narrow, low ceiling roof space. There was already some bedding, dry and clean, usually used by the girl's during the summer, when they chose to sleep there. The large chimney breast rose from the ground floor up through the roof and snuggled beside it there would be some warmth through what was promising to be another bad night.

'Take the ladder against that wall, Herr Szorbá and get the trap door open.' Suddenly spurred on to act, Karl hurried to lift the ladder. Hilde continued asking Esther. 'Do you think you could keep David, quiet enough for me to hide you all up there?' The woman nodded.

'Right, help your wife and child up there,' she ordered Karl who had climbed the ladder pulled back the bolt and let the door fall back against the loft's flooring. Carefully he helped his wife through then handed her the child before following them up into the gloom. Their head reappeared looking down on the woman who had given them this sanctuary.

'I can't give you any light,' Hilde explained craning her neck.' But I'll give you water, bread and cheese and a bucket for ---.' The man his head through the gap nodded understanding.

'--And more honey and herbs for his cough. I'll mix it with chamomile flower tea and a tiny amount of valerian tincture. It will help to calm him.' She had the valerian for her husband when he'd had a seizure and needed to sleep, but a very small amount should do no harm.

'I'm sorry there isn't more I could do. Please be as quiet as you can and as soon as I can I will let you out.'

The man smiled and nodded and waited as Hilde put together the items, wrapped the food in a cloth climbed the ladder and handed it up.

'Now please,' Hilde stood gazing up and wiped her hands on her apron. Outside she could hear the excited chatter of her daughter, and the deeper voice of Josef. They were home together and would need food.

'Close it down and stay until I give a signal.' She didn't wait for a reply, but pulled the ladder away and pushed it along the floor up against the far wall. It would be hard not to glance up to the ceiling and give them away, and she knew the worry would stay with her until they were out of her home and away. It was unlikely Teresa or Leisl would want go up there before the spring, it was so cold and unwelcoming beneath the low roof and the accumulating cobwebs, and Josef hadn't had the energy to climb there in years. Silently the trap door was closed and she breathed a sigh of relief, hoping her face wasn't too flushed enough to give her secret away.

That night after the meal, Josef was tired and went to bed. Once the girl's were settled she followed her husband and tried to sleep. But rest didn't come easy that night. She was conscious of the family of refugees hiding overhead, worried for them and their little boy, and worried the child would cry out with fever and give them away. She fought against the natural instinct to glance towards the ceiling and very nearly fainted when Teresa told her father the next morning during breakfast, about gypsies she'd found in the falling-down barn.

54

Hilde was unusually sharp. 'Don't talk nonsense child,' she rebuked her elder daughter, her voice rising unnecessarily loud.

'Next you will tell us about a *Habergeiss* hiding in the barn waiting to eat little children.' She hoped she was dismissive enough. 'Or,' now Hilde laughed a sound that to her ears sounded false, 'Maybe a *Krampus* has arrived early for Yuletide to find the children who have been misbehaving.'

Teresa's didn't say anything but looked down to the food on her plate, her expression was confused and troubled. Perhaps she had been mistaken, but also hopeful she hadn't really found the terrible *Habergeiss*, the goat bird creature that Gunter had frightened Leisl with more than once, or *Krampus* who he said punished children if they were naughty at Christmas time by taking away all their gifts. She was confused that her mother would say such things but ate her food in silence.

Hilde smiled across the table to her husband, an adult knowing smile, but it seemed Josef thoughts were too preoccupied to take any notice of Teresa's wild imagination.

Chapter 5

Their routine must not alter, not if she was to keep this dreadful secret from her husband.

Early the next morning, leaving Josef in bed, Hilde, Teresa and Leisl walked through the near blizzard, driving a blanket of snow down off the mountains, first to Mass in the tiny church and leaving the girl's to continue on to school. She hurried home, filled with so much dread that the refugees hiding in their roof space had given themselves away and half expecting to find soldiers at their door coming to take them away.

What of Josef? What would he think?

In fear and dread Hilde returned, but the chalet was as she'd left it, silent except for the whistling wind and the muffled sounds coming from the shuttered barn where the irritated hens and goats would have to stay for the rest of the day.

The change in the weather meant it was unlike Josef would go out, unless Herr Mueller drove out in his Steyr 200 motor car and took her father back to the wine hall .

What about the three refugees? Would the Szabós be all right? For all she knew they could have frozen to death overnight and her roof was now filled with corpses.

How she scolded herself for such heinous thoughts and prayed that morning; asking for help and guidance. Her fingers were never far from touching the cross that hung around her neck. She thanked the Lord God, Mary and the child Jesus that there had been no sound from overhead that would have almost certainly given them away. Josef would have noticed or the ever imaginative Teresa.

In the small church earlier, she'd prayed on her knees between her daughters, conscious of the fact that Father Dominic would be expecting her to enter the Confessional at the weekend.

'Help me to keep my secret from my husband and children, so they will be safe. And please show the way to get this poor family to safety. Oh and can you let me know if by telling you this secret in my prayers, it is enough not to tell the Father Dominic put him too, in harm's way?'

Hilde continued to repeat all the novenas she knew in her head over and over again after she left Teresa and Leisl to go to school and she walked towards home.

The wind had dropped and the falling scattering of snow, as the temperature rose slightly, had turned to a steady downpour. If only Josef would be well enough to go and spend time with his friends, she could not visualize a future plan beyond the next hours, and it would give her the opportunity to give her fugitives more food and water, and she could check on David. She could not get the thought from her troubled mind that the surprising quiet could mean the worst: the sick little boy had not survived the night.

For the rest of the day, and over another night, Hilde silently worried. Josef feeling weaker, stayed in bed and slept fitfully as she sewed quietly in front of the fire. Every small, innocent sound made her jumped, whether from her sleeping husband, a branch from a nearby tree banging against a wall or the shifting of logs on the fire. She was convinced any sound would wake her husband and he'd be suddenly suspicious. She sat and stitched and worried: the bread and cheese and water, she'd provided for the hiding family, must have all been eaten by now. They would be hungry and thirsty, and the little boy. How could she check? She longed to put the ladder against the trap door and see they were all right, but commonsense made her fight this rash move and instead she silently prayed for guidance.

The next day was Saturday and God had listened and answered.

The sun was bright and surprisingly warm melting away the last of the snow and drying the ground from the overnight rain. Josef Gŏetschl awoke refreshed from his day of sleep and as often happened had a renewed vigour in his step.

'I shall be spending the day helping Hans replace the side of his barn,' he informed his wife. Hans and Elsa Schultz and their children had the farmstead in the next valley. 'It was blown down during the storm the other night.' The was good news. 'Not that I can do much with my health except hand him the tools and he smiled.

'Don't do too much, darling,' she begged her husband. 'And keep your chest well covered. Perhaps you could take Leisl to play with Corinna and Tomas?' she suggested.

After she kissed them both, she watched and waved them off as they marched over the nearby hill, father and daughter hand in hand, relieved to see her husband looking happy and her little daughter skipping and chatting at his side.

She let a breath out with relief and turned quickly to her oldest daughter sitting watching her. Thank the Good Lord Teresa was a sensible girl for her seven years and she prayed as she had so many times over the last two days, that she could be made to understand the severity of the situation and above all keep the secret.

'I want tell you something that is very important.' She sat her down on the settle next to her and watched her face closely. She could be making a really dreadful mistake, but she trusted her daughter. She might only be seven years of age but she was sensible for someone so young. The child listened as her mother explained about the family in the roof space.

'Can I tell my friend Ingrid.' This was exciting.

'No you must not tell anyone, Teresa. I want you to promise on the Bible, promise to Jesus that you will never tell anyone, ever. Promise.'

Teresa promised, very solemnly on her rosary and then her hand on the Bible her mother took from its place in the cupboard.

'Not even Father Dominic during Confessional, Teresa.' This seemed very wrong to Teresa but she always did as her mother told her, and promised again.

She helped her mother carry the ladder to the trap door and watched as she gently knocked with the broom handle on the trapdoor.

She heard the slight sound of footfall overhead before the door was pulled open and Karl Szabó's face appeared first. It was a face Teresa knew she'd seen before. He looked pale and dirty but thankfully he didn't look as if anything really bad had happened during their long hours of incarceration. As they watched one by one they descended into the room. Of course they were dirty, and hungry, but the best thing of all, David's fever had broken. He looked around with curiosity and smiled a wide grin at Teresa, who ran a finger gently down his thin cheek.

Without many words Teresa and her mother set about making them hot food, while they had a wash in hot water, drying on the thick towels warmed at the fire.

'Thank you Frau,' Karl and Esther were very grateful. 'But now we must go while the weather holds and before your husband returns. You have been kind but we know you are in danger the longer we stay.'

'I did what the Lord wanted me to do,' Hilde replied lifting her chin almost defiantly. She had no arguments with the Jewish nation, but at the back of her mind the Jews had crucified Jesus so maybe her sympathy was as it should be. She'd inwardly wrestled with this dilemma for almost two days, and kept remembering that Christ had preached charity and compassion. And hadn't Jesus himself been born a Jew?

'My husband is a good man,' she defended him, not allowing anyone to question his ways or beliefs.

Karl was saying. 'I am sure he is.'

Hilde changed the subject perhaps quicker than she'd intended. No one would ever be allowed to criticize Josef.

'You have come a long way?' she asked curious overtaking her earlier trepidation.

He hesitated for only a moment. This woman had already done more for his family than was fair to ask in these dangerous times. He trusted her.

'We --- that is myself, Esther and our boy, as well as four more, as an elderly couple and two young men, left our village between Sopron and the AustroHungarian border a week ago. At first we travelled in my shooting brake until we ran out of petrol and by then we were in Austria. We haven't the necessary papers and we couldn't purchase more so had to abandon the car on the road side. We had only our passports sewn into our underclothes. The Wineburgs had been our neighbours. A harmless old couple who only want to get to be with their family. Miriam Wineberg has a bad heart and we tried to find her, the younger men took it in turns to carry her but even after a short way it became too much for the old lady so we had to give up. We rested behind bushes on the side of a dirt path when a farmer with horse and cart drove by. Frau Wineberg was sick by then so her husband offered the farmer their jewellery if he would take them to the nearest doctor or hospital. We all knew they were at the mercy of the farmer and that he could just as easily hand them over to the German authorities. But Frau Wineberg is very frail and her husband took the risk the farmer would be kind.'

Esther snorted, a strange sound coming from such a small woman.

'Kind! Karl, I didn't trust that farmer. I said so. He would take from them all their possessions and leave them on the road side or worse. We have no way of knowing if they got to a hospital or even if they are still alive.'

Her husband reached and touched her hand. 'I know. I know, but what else could we do Esther? The Winebergs are old and tired and frightened. We did what we could and we prayed for their safety.'

'Hmm. They should have stayed with us.' Esther Szabó set her mouth in a strong line and pulled her son closer.

'The two young men Mika and Yanni, both in their twenties, travelled with us,' continued Karl ignoring his wife. 'I know they came from a town close to our village, but not much more about them except they talked of getting to Yugoslavia and joining up with some communists or partisans.'

'Hush, husband,' scolded the cautious Esther. 'You say too much.'

'We have placed our trust in Frau Göetschl so far and she has the right to know our story.'

Again he ignored her distrust and the stern expression on her face.

'After we said our goodbyes to the Winebergs, we continued on foot. We hid during the days in woods and derelict farm buildings or anything that looked safe and kept moving southwest during the night. We didn't know anyone we could trust and so we avoided people as much as possible. There were the odd German patrols and troop movements but we didn't encounter that many on the smaller roads through the country. The night time was very cold and we soon ran out of food, but hiding in woods we took the risk of lighting fires and Yanni was very skilled at catching rabbits and foraging for anything Esther could cook.

We are hoping to get to Switzerland. We must do what we can to get across the border. I have family living in Geneva. My brother will be in a car on the mountain pass in Switzerland. He'll wait for an hour tonight and then again tomorrow night. After that he will assume we haven't made it that far.'

Teresa watched the boy as he took a piece of bread from his mother and nibble on the golden crust and then emptied the mug of the rich goats milk, milked early that morning when she'd collected the eggs and let the animals out of the barn. She was fascinated by the family who'd been living above and no one except her mother had known about them. Would Liesl and herself have been able to stay so quiet for so long? She didn't think so.

Hilde was speaking. 'You have quite a way to go yet. If you go by the roads it will take you two or three hours to get to the border and then there is the high mountain ridge to get over. Also the soldiers from the barracks in the north often patrol the roads during the night.' Hilde pointed towards the south. 'It would be quickest to go through the forest. But unless you know its terrain, it is easy to get lost and lose your bearings. There are many dangers even if you could find your way during the day light never mind in the dark. There is a narrow pass between two hills that would cut down on the distance but again that area would probably be patrolled.'

Karl nodded looking glum. 'I see.'

She would know about this place and he knew he was putting so much faith and trust in this woman. If she'd intended to turn them over to the German's she'd have done that already. So what she was saying made sense but didn't help him save his family. Hadn't the little girl found them hiding in the barn? And the mother had risked her own safety to give them warmth and food, and helped with David's recovery. He wondered how he would ever be able to repay their kindness never mind what he was planning now.

Teresa liked David, he was still looking a little weak but he had large dark eyes and a shy smile. She found an old wooden horse her father had made for her when she was small, and gave it to him. The child clasped it to his hollow chest and snuggled into his mother. Esther smiled her thanks.

'Where are the young men now?' Hilde suddenly asked.

'We were separated a few kilometers from here. We came upon a group of army vehicles and patrol on the road at running alongside the river ---,' he pointed to the valley to the north. 'Yanni and Mika suddenly took off running into the woods and it gave us the chance to escape before we were spotted. The soldiers gave chase and we hid until the coast was clear. We could hear shouting and gun fire at first then nothing. We don't know what happened to them, but we just kept going.'

Karl gazed away and out through the window. Teresa was sure she saw tears in his eyes.

'We hope and pray,' said Esther, holding her child close, 'they got away. They were very brave,---- but we just don't know.'

'So,' said Karl with sudden determination. 'We must go now, before we put you and your family in more danger.'

Hilde didn't argue or suggest they return to the comparative safety of the roof space. Teresa watched as her mother stood and started to gather together bread and fruit and place them into a cloth bag.

'I'll give you food and,' she looked critically at their clothes now ripped and shabby with holes and torn seams. She was brisk and business-like.

'My husband's old coat should fit you, and Frau Szorbá you can wear one of my dresses and tie a shawl around your head. I have nothing for the boy, but a shawl around him will help keep out the biting wind. They will disguise ---.' She stopped speaking but busied herself gathering together the items.

She didn't say it but explanation was unnecessary. These offered clothes were more in keeping with people of the Gőetschl status and not the obvious fine wool and expensive materials of their clothes. They would blend in more easily. Esther was grateful. 'Thank you.'

They washed and changed and not only were they brighter physically but their moods had lifted.

'Just to make sure,' she instructed her daughter. 'Go and get the crucifix and rosaries from the drawer. And you'll find the armbands in the cupboard. Go on child.'

She saw Karl glance nervously at the photograph on the wall. It was the Hitler photo that no matter where one was in the room, the small cold eyes seem to follow.

'I know you don't want to wear these things but please they may protect you if you are stopped. You haven't papers but you have your passports safely stitched into your undergarments, but outwardly you must appear to be a peasant like me. No, no please.'

She refused to listen to any contradiction.

'If you are wearing the Star of David on your persons then hide them with the passports and in plain sight each of you wear a crucifix and carry a rosary.' She hardly glanced at the antique gold crucifix that had once belonged to her grandmother. She knew she would never see it again, but it was unimportant.

'Put the armbands on your sleeves so any soldier can see them.'

She watched as they silently did her bidding.

'My family has lived beside the forest all our lives, so we know it well. I'll guide you through the deepest part and to the gap that leads out towards the valley and then beyond across the low hills towards the border. It is a little used pass through the mountains. Although impassable during winter there hasn't been enough snow to block it yet, so you should be able to get through. There are one or two places, small hills and groups of trees that will give you some cover. After I show you the way beyond the forest, I'm sorry I won't be able help you further.'

Karl listened, his brow furrowed.

'So. There shouldn't be soldiers in the forest? The danger will be out in the open across the valley towards the mountains, once we leave the forest cover.'

Hilde nodded her head and unconsciously straightened the cross now hanging around the boys neck.

'I can only go by their routine up to now. The last time the German's sent the men and dogs into the forest was two years ago when there was a rumour a gypsy band was camping in the east.'

'So we must be vigilant until we reach safety,' confirmed Esther.

'Yes. I shall walk some way ahead of you in case there is something wrong and I'll carry a basket that I'll start to fill with mushrooms, wild berries and garlic. It's something we do at this time of year and the patrol would not think it unusual to find someone foraging. It's what we do. Most of the German guards know my husband. I don't think they would stop me.'

'There is always the first time,' commented Karl.

'Yes,' said Hilde quietly. 'There is always the first time. Keep a distance but not so far you lose me and at the first sign of something wrong find someplace to hide. This time of the year the forest floor is covered in pine needles, shrubs, bracken and dead tree branches.'

'Yes. And the last thing anyone must do is panic,' said Karl wisely. 'The worst thing would be to run. We will all be in danger.'

Hilde felt rejuvenated as if her God had given her an important task and she intended to do it to the best of her ability. He would look after them and get them to safety, this she was absolutely convinced.

For the first time Teresa sensed this was not some grown up game.

'*Mutti*,' she asked in a loud whisper as she hurried to do her mother's bidding. 'Why are we in danger? Are there bad people looking for David and his *vater und mutti*?'

Hilde sighed. Was she putting too much responsibility on a seven year olds shoulders?

'I'll tell you all about it later, *leibchen*. Now you will stay here and wait for me to return. You must be patient because it will take a few hours. If your father and Leisl come home before me give them the stew from the pan on the stove. There is freshly baked bread. Tell *Vater* I have gone foraging in the forest.'

It was best if she was to tell as near to the truth as possible.

'Remember your promise. You must not tell him about David and his parents. Understand.'

Teresa nodded and her mother took her by her arms and made her face her.

'Do you understand, Teresa? You made a promise to keep this a secret forever and never tell anyone. You promised Jesus.'

Teresa's bottom lip quivered at her mother's sudden unexplained sternness.

'Yes *Mutti*. I understand.'

Hilde let her daughter go and pulled her into her arms.

'You are a good, obedience child and I love you, *mein leibchen*.'

Chapter 6

They heard the car before they saw it. It was driving ever closer and Hilde recognized the engine. They had to move fast.

It was Henrich Mueller. He must have known Josef was out for the day.

'Quickly. Someone's coming.'

There was no time to get up to the roof space. He would be here at her door in a couple of minutes. If they moved now they could get out along the side wall and to the little used rear door of the old barn. That door was hardly used these days and might be overgrown, and the door catch rusted into the lock, but it wasn't padlocked like the double front doors. It was the best she could come up with, and the good thing was her landlord never went near the barn.

'But *Mutti* ---,' Teresa was about to object. It was only the fat mayor and he would help them. Couldn't he take them to the border in his car? That would be nice for David, him being so sick, and he could ride in the front seat.

'No. No. Teresa don't argue. Please child, do as I say. Go to the barn with Herr and Frau Szabó and keep as quiet as you can. Stay there until I come to get you. Go Now.'

The four, speedily gathered together the items that had been prepared to take with them and as the sound of the car's engine drew closer they snuck out the door alongside the chalet out of sight of the approaching car and into the barn. The hens clucked and ran off while the goats, curious, hung around the door hoping for food. The rear single door was stiff and objected to the urgent wrenching, as Karl struggled to get it open.

He managed to pull it from its warped frame as he heard the car pull up around the front. They were hidden from sight as they hurried inside and he pulled the door to. Teresa and the family hid in the semi-dark finding bales of straw to sit on and David and Teresa played with the wooden horse as the adults sat nervously waiting. No one said very much.

The big black car pulled up and Heinrich, with all the confidence and power he felt his position gave him, strutted towards the open doorway. From the open doorway, the aroma of food: a pan of stew perhaps bubbling on the stove. The smell made him slaver. The food smelt good and as he walked towards the woman stirring over the pan, his appetite broadened.

Hilde Gőetschl was still a beautiful woman. Her head bent as if she hadn't heard him arrive, revealed fine, downy hair growing on the nape of her neck. Her firm shoulders and straight back leading to a slim waist and well-shaped hips. She turned towards him as he moved closer, and his eyes travelled down her lovely features to her throat and down to heavily rounded breasts. Even in a dress, plain and drab in its muddy colour, something his Clara would not have been seen dead in, Hilde was a magnificent specimen of womanhood. As the most important bureaucrat in the town he made it his business to always know what was going on, and he knew she was alone for the day. Josef and the girl's were otherwise engaged until the evening.

'Hilde,' he spoke her name low but heavy with desire. 'You're alone?'

Hilde turned, as if surprised at his arrival, and tried to find a smile. The corners of her mouth turned up but the smile was forced, and she was suddenly finding it hard to breathe. He was one side of the pine table watching her, and even from this distance she felt the bile rise in her throat at sight of his bloated fleshy cheeks and thick red lips. His large presence seemed to fill the room and she clenched her fists at her waist fighting against the need to faint. This was not the time to lose her nerve.

'Heinrich. My husband isn't home.'

'Yes I know. That's why I've come now.'

'But we don't need more medication ---.'

He laughed but it wasn't a sound that filled her with relief. He was laughing at her naivety and she knew had no other option but to do his bidding. She had to think not just of her family, her husband and her daughters, but the real danger waiting for her to act hiding in the barn a few steps away. This man would not hesitate in handing them into his new found colleagues and friends. It would be in his best interest to have Josef arrested no matter how much of a friend he appeared to be. Everything he did, his every thought was aimed at seeing more of Hilde, she had been his obsession since they were young and she had turned him down for Josef. This had seared in his consciousness every day since. He had to have this beautiful woman before him and no one would stand in his way.

'What do you want, Heinrich?' she asked him quietly knowing the answer.

He stepped around the table and towards her until all he had to do was reach out his arms.

'I want you.'

She knew she was lost and repulsed, but made her reluctant body relax into his arms as he pulled her into a tight embrace and buried his face into her neck. She stopped herself from crying out as his hand moved under her skirt and up her leg.

'Please God,' she prayed. 'Don't let Teresa come in now.'

Chapter 7

'How much longer is that man going to stay?' Karl muttered the question for the second time. He'd traded his gold pocket watch for a glass of milk for David a few days before. The woman at the rundown farmhouse had been only too pleased to give this man a glass from the pail in exchange for this valuable timepiece, and although it had belonged to his grandfather, his son was too precious for its loss to matter. It had only been ten minutes but it felt a lot longer and he had no idea how long it would take to get to the border especially if they had to avoid any troops.

Esther shrugged. Whatever was happening inside the chalet she kept to herself sensing that to keep everyone safe, Hilde was doing what was necessary but she felt a great sadness for the sacrifice. Could she have done the same in such circumstances? She didn't know.

'We could try and get through the forest before the light goes,' she suggested wrapping the shawl tighter around her little son's thin body. He was still weak and their journey was not yet over. Perhaps they were about to embark on the most dangerous journey so far?

'And we could get lost or end up shot. We would have no idea of direction and could end up going round and round in circles and miss the rendezvous with Isaac. On the Swiss side he will wait only a short time then leave. It wouldn't be safe to hang around'

'So what's the answer? How long is that man going to stay and we need Frau Gőetschl as our guide?'

It was as if she had been forgotten and Teresa stayed silent until: 'I can show you the way through the forest. I know the way.'

The man and woman turned to face her and Teresa lifted her chin with youthful confidence.

'Leisl and me, we have always gone with *Mutti* to pick mushrooms and we often play in the forest. I know all the best hiding places. '

Esther shook her head. 'No. No Teresa.'

Her husband agreed. 'This is not a game of hide and seek.'

'The longer we stay here the more dangerous it is for you and your sister, your mother and father,' said the woman.

Through the gap in the door frame she could see the line of trees, the wall of tall trunks at the edge reaching into the pale blue November sky. They seemed so near: once in their embrace she hoped would be the beginning of the end to this week long nightmare. But she knew deep down this was deception and they were still so far away from safety.

'Karl,' her voice was low and held a note of panic, as if in saying his name she had finally revealed the terror she'd held tightly inside.

He saw her fear deep in her eyes and touching her head and his son's face stood with renewed determination.

'Come. We will go now before it gets too late in the afternoon.'

Teresa also stood ready to leave the barn but the man stopped her.

'No. You will stay in the here until your mother comes for you. We will leave through the rear door and keep close to the house wall until we can take make for that group of trees just beyond. Please thank her for her kindness and explain we had to go. She is a very brave woman.'

The old woman bent forward to ease her deformed foot back into the shoe and the sudden sharp pain in her chest made her gasp. She should be moving but it was pleasant just sitting reminiscing. The day felt almost as chilled as it had on that afternoon seventy-one years before and she felt as proud of her Mutti even now after all that time. She not understood her mother's sacrifice until much later, but what she'd done to safe them God had ultimately forgiven that particular sin.

And suddenly she recalled as clear as day the way as a seven year old waiting impatiently in that old falling-down barn she'd stood and faced the two strangers, her stance determined and stubborn.

'I can do it. I can show you the way through the forest and across the valley.'

Had she stamped her foot with childish, precocious frustration? Probably.

'I can do it,' she repeated. 'I won't let you and David down. I really do know all the best places to hide.'

Karl looked down at his feet and moved the straw around the dry wooden floor with the dusty toe of his boot, while Esther slowly shook her head. She could see the worry deep in her husband's eyes and sense the urgency in his stooped shoulders.

'No Karl. She's a child. And it's not right to involve her anymore. We either wait until Frau Gőetschl gets rid of that man and he drives away --- or we go now, and take our chances.'

Her husband didn't speak but thought not for the first time how upside down their world had become. They had had a good life, living in a nice house with friends close by and leaving each morning to go to drive to his office ten kilometers away. Suddenly they'd been targeted and terrorized by people and neighbours because of their creed, and they and others had

had to flee for their lives. It didn't make sense. He sighed deeply. Nothing in this sad, mad world made sense anymore.

He looked first at his son as resting now against his mother's chest he was falling asleep, then at his wife.

'I don't know what else to do Esther,' he rubbed trembling fingers across his eyes. 'We have come so far and the border feels so close.'

Without answering his wife handed him the sleeping boy and picked up their bag holding their meager belongings and walked purposefully the couple of steps to the rear door of the barn. She carefully pulled it open alarmed at the creaking sound it made, but her own commonsense telling her it couldn't be overheard above the sound of the wind in the rafters and the creaking of the old wooden building. Karl followed her into the sharp clear air and they stood together carefully looking around and into the distance that would take them to the edge of the forest. On this blind side of the barn one or two hens clucked, and fussed, pecking around in the dirt at their feet. There was no other sound.

The two didn't look back as nervously they hugged the wooden wall and then the rear of the chalet until there was no other option but to take their chances and sprint towards a crop of stones naturally piled, closed by.

It felt so furtive, so overly dramatic as they crouched low and ran across the small patch of open were they felt as exposed as if sudden appearing naked in their crowded market place back home. Home. They would never see their homeland again and not for the first time Esther Szabó had to fight back ready tears.

The line of trees seemed so close, but the distance was deceptive. Neither dared to look back towards the chalet and the barn that had been their safe place for a few days. They knew the man still had to be inside they would have heard his car drive off. It seemed such a long time ago since they'd had to make a hasty departure, but in reality it was only about fifteen to twenty minutes. The longer he stayed inside the more chance they had to get clear, because they wouldn't be seen until he drove away from the building and along the narrow open track back towards the town.

Karl moved his sleeping son to his other shoulder and wrapped the shawl tighter around the boy. His wife close behind him nudged his arm and together they ran keeping as close to the edge of the valley and along the under hang of moss covered rocks. Out of breath and shaking with fear they didn't stop until they were only meters away from the trees. From leaving the relative shelter of the barn it had taken them longer than they'd first imagined. Distance was an illusion.

They were in shadow cast by the giant trees and stopped to get their breath and their bearings.

They had got this far without sudden shouts of 'halt', or guns being fired.

'Which way?' Esther asked taking David from his father as he stirred and looked around with eyes wide with wonder. He tightly held the carved wooden horse.

'I think we must try and keep going to the left,' answered her husband trying to peer into the sudden blackness. There appeared very little light that actually penetrated the dense closely growing mass. 'Keep going left and sooner or later we should come out to the south. We have no way of knowing just how big this forest is but can it really be that big if Teresa and her sister are allowed to play inside.'

Esther wasn't that sure but kept quiet.

It was a few nervous steps as they entered the packed claustrophobic atmosphere of the Alpine pine forest. A few more steps and the wind high in the trees but partially muffled by the thick growth of branches made the place eerie and unreal. But the forest has its own sounds and as they moved further into its interior they heard the scurrying of small animals in the undergrowth and birdsong high above their heads. Beneath their feet was a thick carpet of rotting needles and gnarled branches, cones crunched under their shoes. The scent of pine resin and the earthy smell of rotting vegetation: heady and overpowering. In their home land they had visited woods and forests, in better times taking picnics and marveling at the insects, squirrels and mindful of the wild boar that roamed, but they had never been in a forest that was so dense and felt so alien.

A movement behind them and Karl spun round expecting the worst. A small figure, her braided hair tangled and falling loose, a shawl tied tightly around her shoulders and clutching the basket, stood half hidden behind the thick trunk of a tree.

'Teresa,' his voice louder than he'd intended made her start and he thought she was going to turn and run back the way she'd come.

'I followed you,' she hesitated unsure of the man and woman's reaction. 'You'll get lost unless I show you the way.'

The woman shocked, put a hand to her mouth. 'Oh dear God, child. You must go home to your mother. She will be so worried.'

Teresa stood firm. 'Look in my basket, I have picked some mushrooms.' She tipped the wicker basket to show her small harvested bounty and tentatively took a step closer. A large bird, started, flew up from a high branch squawking in annoyance. Not too far away an owl called probably getting ready for an early evening of hunting for a meal.

'Teresa.' The boy struggled in his mother's arms, demanding to be set down so he could show his new friend he still clutched the toy she'd given him.

Teresa bent to touch the boys head and then taking his offered hand in hers, said. 'I can show the way.'

The boy and girl walked resolutely passed the man and woman and Esther looked with despair, but her husband shrugged and followed.

For seconds she stood, uncertain and scared. The only sensible thing to do was to take the girl back to her mother and hope they could still escape before the German's found them, but where was sense these days? She could hear the girl chatting and singing a lullaby to her son.

Sleep, baby sleep.
The father herds the sheep.
The mother shakes a little tree,
Down falls a little dream.
Sleep, baby sleep.

It made her yearn for the life she knew was over forever. She followed the sound of the children as the forest's heavy shade enveloped her.

Mrs Teresa Hunt watched as a plump well fed cat slinked along the edge of the grass passed her feet and then sprang up onto the facing bench. It sat and for a few seconds stared at the old woman before it began the leisurely intense task of having a wash. She hummed a tune of a long forgotten lullaby, and if she tried really hard she might even remember some of the words to the song her mother had sung to her and she had sung to the boy David as they walked further into that forest that after noon so long ago. The words were faltering and she could only think of them in German: it was too much of an effort to translate in her tired mind.

Schlaf, Kindlein schlaf,
Der Vater hut die Schaf.
Die Mutter schuttelts Baumelein
Da fallt herab ein Traumelein.
Schlaf, Kindlein schlaf.

She sighed. It had been a long time, sixty years since she'd heard or spoken her native tongue and she knew she'd never again.

As he had predicted Karl, his wife and the two children kept moving to the left. Only occasionally was there any sign of a track and only narrow enough to have been a natural path for an animal, probably deer, snuffling in the undergrowth for the young shoots. For the most part the forest was enclosing and importantly made them feel invisible.

Chapter 8

She didn't speak at all, her shame and most of all the feeling of violation making her stomach churn. So much shame, yet he had forced himself on her and she'd not been able to stop him, he was so much stronger and any attempt to reason had made only heightened his passion.

Hilde Gőetschl sat very still on the edge of her marital bed clasping her hands tightly in her lap. She fought down the desire to vomit as only minutes before she'd had to endure his probing hands on her naked body, her clothes ripped in pile on the floor, his foul breath on her face and mouth.

Heinrich Mueller was pleased with himself. He'd always known Hilde would be his one day. He re-arranged his clothing and continued to pontificate on his most important role as town's major and chief of police and how he was privy to Claus's most secret orders as if it had been a normal visit.

'My good friend Oberführer Claus Schmit, told me of the two men, two Communists,' he mimicked the brash pompous way of the man he so admired and would have given anything to emulate given the chance.

'A few days ago they were attempting to flee to the north to fight against our troops.'

It was only right and proper he thought of the German army as part of Austria and he lifted his chin and squared his shoulders, in a manner of standing to attention, almost unconsciously.

'The soldiers tracked them down of course,' his self righteous chuckle was more a snort. 'One was shot dead before he could be captured and interrogated, and unfortunately his friend escaped.'

He adjusted his braces and then reached for his coat and hat flung over Josef's chair.

'But be assured he'll not get far. So far the patrols have been combing the area and concentrating on the woods to the east, but have now turned their attention to the large forest to the south east of this place. Don't worry he is of no threat to you and your family, the dog will be caught. The commandant thinks he'll be trying to get across one of the borders, during the next couple of days and nights. That's where they'll track him down and hopefully shoot him for the traitor he is.'

Still praising the work of his German friends and the local Nazi stronghold, Mueller left with a proud self-satisfied bounce to his step. To his mind all was right with his world, as he forced his bulk into the driving seat of his shiny black car and drove off.

As if awaking from a traumatic nightmare Hilde blinked hard and took a deep breath before straightening the bed covers. This was not the time to break down and scream her heart out with self pity. She filled the sink with hot water from the kettle and proceeded to systematically scrub her body from feet to hair until her skin was red raw. She dressed quickly then, after fingering her Rosary and offering a prayer for forgiveness for the sin she had just committed, but it had been her sin to allow it to happen, and she confirmed Mueller hadn't suddenly returned or her husband and child weren't on their way home. She rushed down the short path, scattering hens in front of her to one side in her haste, to the half opened door of the barn. Any regret for what she'd done and betrayal of her marriage vows she needed to put to one side for now. She could concentrate on redeeming herself in the eyes of God when she knew everyone was safe. Hilde couldn't dismiss what Mueller had just told her and she repeated a 'thank you God', that without knowing it he had saved them from making a tragic and potentially fatal mistake in escaping through the forest.

'Herr Szabó, Frau, Teresa,' she called them in a low voice as if unconsciously she still feared of being overheard and discovered.

No movement. No answer. The barn was still, only dust and small particles of straw swam and danced in the shallow beam of weak sunlight filtered through the gap.

Hilde's heart was thumping in her chest and suddenly she was finding it had to breathe as realization sent bile into her mouth.

Oh dear God. The barn was empty. As she stepped further inside her eyes grew accustomed to the gloom and she saw the small, unused rear door was slightly ajar. The family had gone, but where was Teresa?

'Teresa. Teresa.' Her voice rose with renewed terror.

Had they taken her with them? Had they forced her seven year old daughter to go with them and show them the way to escape? How could they do this awful thing? She'd been kind to them, shown them charity and compassion and they had taken her precious daughter.

Hilde was beside herself with horror. The soldiers could track them down and they were 'the undesirables' as were the two Communists they would shoot them dead --- and Teresa was with them.

Oh dear God, Mary mother of God. Jesus, please not that.

She could hardly see through the tears and the sobs that choked her as she ran out of the barn, down the shallow valley and towards the great bank of tall trees that edged the mass.

'Teresa,' she yelled, cupping her hands around her mouth now dry with a fear so horrifying her tongue seemed swollen to twice its size and she was finding it hard to force out her daughter's name.

Again and again, in one direction then the next but the name rebounded back off the bark of so many tightly packed trees and seemed to mock her.

Which way would they have gone? Should she try to follow? But as someone who had spent her life living close to this majesty of nature, she understood and respected and was daunted by how easy it was to get lost if panicked. She could go off after her daughter and because of her fear just as easily get herself lost without thinking it out clearly. Lost or captured, or worse. The only thing that was a speck of comfort was that her children had played amongst the trees almost as soon as they could walk. The forest was Teresa and Leisl's natural playground. But that had been when their lives weren't in terrible danger and in summer time with the sun blazing through the canopy overhead and not a chilling dull day in late autumn.

She took note the sun was already low in the sky, a large red globe radiating minimal heat yet hovering and shimmering just above the distant mountains. Already the day was growing colder promising a freezing night once dark.

Taking a few steps beyond the first straggling trees, into the shadowy darkness of the forest, she cupped her mouth once more and shouted.

'Teresa.'

It was then, that to her left and far beyond her presence, she heard the two muffled sounds of gunshots.

Esther sensed the danger first. It was the very gentle sound of rustling quite close by: that was possibly just a small animal foraging for berries in the undergrowth to their left. It was becoming harder to see more that a short distance in front, and with very few breaks or clearing to stop and catch their breath and try to get their bearings. She was walking close to her husband while David followed closely on the little girl's booted heels still clutching the toy horse as if it was now his most treasured possession, and perhaps it was good that such a small, roughly hewn item could give him security at a time like this. They moved slowly and cautiously and she could hear her man taking deep gulps of air as if frightened to breathe in case he alone could threaten their immediate safety. They didn't speak, but every inch of their being was concentrating on their survival. Only the child Teresa, too young for such a responsibility walked through the trees along a path she seemed to know and recognize, with almost too much confidence for her years.

'Karl,' Esther hissed his name as a voice, the words unclear but still managing to sound clipped and authoritive, broke the relative silence and sent a flock of small startled birds flying high from the branches overhead.

'Quick. David ---.' Esther pulled her son to the side into a thicket of bracken and undergrowth made into a small hill by season upon season of pine needles and leaves. Karl moved as quick into bushes close by and the three lay low, as low as they possibly could. Teresa took seconds longer to realize why David and his parents were no longer following but had no more time than to hide her slim figure behind a thick trunk of a towering tree before the two soldiers appeared as shadows from the right.

'I'm sure I saw something,' said one poking the bayonet on the end of his rifle into the nearest pile of leaves.

'Probably a deer or could be a boar. Do you think there are many boars in here?'

His friend was idly piercing the ground with the bayonet with little enthusiasm and yawned deeply. This had been a long tiring day and he would welcome a meal and his bed in the overfilled barracks.

'Could be,' he would have some fun at his friend's expense. 'Look. Over there.' He brought up his rifle to his shoulder.' I'm sure I saw a furry thing moving over there.' He fired once then again. Karl and his wife jumped at the sudden sound so close and David gave a cry until his mother covered his mouth with her hand and held him even closer to keep him still.

Teresa behind the tree gasped in alarm. She didn't dare move. Her legs felt all wobbly.

The young soldier laughed and punched his friend's shoulder with delight. 'Only a squirrel. I was only joking Franz.'

But Franz was angry at being made a fool of. This was a serious business. A traitor to the Reich was trying to escape. He prodded angrily at the ground at his feet then moved to another area of the clearing to a small rise of fallen and rotting mulch.

The second man shrugged his shoulders. Franz was too serious, too fanatical always praising the Führer and the Party instead of having fun. But he followed his example and found a mound of strong smelling undergrowth to poke and prod.

Karl was sweating with horror. The long, lethal blade was only inches from his wife and child. What could he do? He couldn't bear it. As if it had already happened he could almost hear the blade slicing through his beloved Esther's flesh and David, his darling boy, he must not die at the hands of these fiends.

'What are you doing?'

The two soldiers spun round, their rifle aimed in the direction of the voice. A girl stood half hidden behind a tree. At her feet was a basket on its side, its contents of mushrooms and berries had scattered on the ground.

Teresa stood as straight and as still as she could, but the men with those pointy knifes pointing at her frightened her.

'I --- I was picking mushrooms. *Mutti* said I must pick as many as I can before the animals get to them.'

'Little girl,' one had recovered his surprise, but he still stared at her suspicious. The British were underhand and crafty like the fox. It was quite likely they recruited small children to fight. 'You should not be here in the forest.' He moved closer and scrutinized her small person. She was wearing a woolen coat, mittens and boots, and across her shoulders and the neck of the coat was tied a hand-woven shawl in bright reds and blues. Her clothes were dirty and the hem of her coat had a small rip where she had caught it on brambles. Her boots were scuffed and her small face grubby. The shawl obviously previously tied around her head, had slipped and her one brown plait had escaped from the coronet curling around her small head.

Franz from Berlin, lowered his weapon and clicked his tongue with annoyance. 'It's one of the *gassenjung* I've seen in the town.'

The old woman chuckled at the memory. A ragamuffin he had called her. Yes, she probably had looked very untidy and dirty by then. Had Mutti been angry at the state of her clothes when she got home? She couldn't remember.

'I can show you were to pick the very best mushrooms if you'd like,' she said as she stooped to retrieve her harvest from the forest's floor and put them back in her basket.'

Franz's friend relaxed and pulled a packet of cigarettes out of his tunic's breast pocket. Placing his rifle on the ground at his feet he lit the end with a lighter.

'Let her go. She's harmless.' Dropping the match on the ground he dragged deeply on the cigarette letting the smoke drift from his nostrils like dragon's breath, or that's how Teresa saw it.

'*Mutti* says I have to fill the basket before I can go home.'

That was a terrible lie and she mused at just how many 'hail Mary's' she'd have to say.

Karl, with Esther and their son only a short distance away, all three covered in molding vegetation was fearful of what would happen next. Thankfully his wife and child were managing to keep very still while this was happening, but the slightest movement would give their position away. The girl could so easily give them up to the Germans, maybe not even on purpose but by looking furtively in their direction or saying the wrong thing. He found himself grasping the crucifix he been advised to wear by Frau Gőetschl earlier, tightly in his fist.

This child was amazing and Esther admiration went out to her even though in some ways it was a foolish thing to do. Teresa, the basket's handle now in the crook of an elbow, stood very straight and faced the men with a frustrated expression on her face.

'Well. Do you want me to show you were to find the mushrooms or not?'

Karl heard himself drawing in his breath through clenched teeth. Had she gone too far? The young soldiers in their severe dark uniforms, helmets and those menacing rifles might get annoyed and could shoot her and dispose of her body in the undergrowth. No one would know or even care about the disappearance of a girl, except her family. Except Karl and Esther, and David. He must save her, even at the knowledge he would have to give himself and his family away to an uncertain future: if any future at all. But what else could he do?

Franz's comrade suddenly laughed.

'Go home little girl. Go back to your mother and tell her there are no mushrooms in the forest today.'

Franz nodded. '*Ja. Go. Go. Schnell.*' He waved this rifle in her direction and Teresa's nerve failed her. She turned and ran back the way she'd come, dropping the basket contents once again. This time she didn't stop to pick them up.

Chapter 9

'Oh God. Oh God.'

Hilde didn't know what to do. The sound of firing had turned her to stone as she'd stood on the edge of the forest. Had they been shooting at her child? Had they hit her? She could be lying amongst the fallen needles, badly injured or worse? Where was she? How could she find her? The forest was so vast to search on her own. She had some idea the direction Teresa and the Szabó's might have taken, but she could easily take the wrong turning, every tree and bush looked the same as another. She was finding it impossible to think of what to do next. She couldn't think or reason a plan.

Hilde sat on the rise of a hillock close by and winding her arms around herself rocked backwards and forwards. What a terrible day it had been. How could Jesus allow this to happen?

Teresa didn't run very far. Once out of sight she stepped behind a tree and then very carefully edged back the way she'd come until still in the protection of one of the mighty trees she could sneak a look towards the clearing. She wasn't close enough to hear what they said, but could see Franz from Berlin, the soldier who'd spoken to her and her friends on that day, and his friend just finishing his cigarette, standing in the centre. He flicked the cigarette carelessly into the shrubs and then shouldering their rifles, started to walk away.

Except for the irritating buzzing of minute insects in the trees and the occasional animal sound, it was silent and as if by mutual understanding the four stayed still and quiet for sometime after the men left.

Taking a chance, it was Karl who stood first, shaking and brushing off the debris, then moving to help up his wife and David. David was whimpering, his eyes wide with fear. He'd not understood why his mother had made him stay under all those smelly leaves with her hand over his mouth, but he sensed it was better to have ants crawling over his leg, than to struggle or cry out.

They anxiously look about at the densely packed trees. They had no idea which way to go. In fact they couldn't have found their way back towards the valley and their recent refuge if they'd attempted to. There was no point of reference, no tree stump or twisted branch that would help them get their bearings. And as the seconds ticked by, there was always the terror that the men with rifles and fixed bayonets could come back. Esther shivered and by natural reflex lifted her son into her arms and held him close. Sensing his wife's new fear he put an arm around her shoulders and she nestled her head into his neck.

'What now Karl?' she whispered. 'How do we find our way out of this and meet Isaac?' She was close to tears and Karl had no answer for his young wife.

'It's not far now.'

The voice made them jump, and turning round they found their little guide standing on the edge of the clearing.

'We thought you'd gone,' said Esther surprised, then as her natural maternal instinct took over, she semi scolded with. 'You should have gone back home, child. Your mother will be sick with worry.'

Teresa stood swinging her empty basket and a cheeky, childish grin that lit up her small face and highlighted the dirty streak on her chin.

'I only pretended, when Franz from Berlin told me to, then I hid.' She added proud of her achievement, 'I can find really good hidey holes.'

Karl was worried. It had to be quite late in the afternoon and dusk would be soon. How far to the meeting point where his brother had said he'd be waiting? Could they ask this child to do more as real danger was so near?

Teresa was growing bored with the indecision of the adult and without another word, walked past them and through a partially hidden gap in the trees. She expected they'd follow her and pursing her lips she was satisfied to hear the rustle of the leaves under their feet indicating they were close on her heels. She was supremely confident. She thought she knew every tree in the forest and she and her sister had often played here in on the hot summer days, and not once had they got themselves lost. She had a natural sense of direction although Teresa would have known to give her gift a title, only aware that if she'd ever lost her little sister in the forest she would have been in big trouble with her parents.

How long they kept going? Karl had no idea. He had taken his weary son in his arms and even such a slight weight seemed to be as heavy as lead in arms that were aching from tiredness and stress. If anything the trees seemed to be getting thicker with less space between their old trunks, their low branches stretching out to entangle with neighbouring branches and overgrown soft fruit bushes with sharp angry barbs.

Then as Esther stumbled once again, her legs not wanting to take another step, and even the girl just ahead of them slowing and dragging her feet, the trees appeared to be thinning. As they skirted a clump of scrubby brambles, the setting sun shone like a beacon temporarily blinding them all. The sun was just to their right, setting in the west so they were certainly facing the border.

They stood for only minutes breathing and gulping in air as if they'd been denied oxygen for the past hours.

Karl set David on the ground and Teresa stooped to touch his soft cheek with a finger. He grabbed her hand and at the same time tightened his hold on the wooden horse: he wanted to hold his new friend's hand but was afraid she would want his toy back.

'You can have that, David,' she assured him. 'So you always remember me.'

Karl gazed forward. In front was flat scrub land unfarmed and wild. Another small wood, with deciduous trees now almost bare of their red and gold foliage and easy to skirt, towards a shallow bank of low-lying hills. Beyond he could see the misty mountains that presumably were the way they had to go to final sanctuary.

Teresa pointed with her mitten covered hand.

'There.'

'That will lead to the pass that will take us to the Swiss border?' asked Esther.

The girl nodded, her attention back on the boy tightly holding her other hand.

Karl wanted to move. They were still in danger. There was no knowing how many German's were close by patrolling this part of the forest. He was sweating with nerves and eagerness. So close to safety he could almost taste it.

'Come on. Hurry.'

The next step was in the open, however small, it was a dangerous area to be exposed in. Once across that flat bit of land and into the relative shade of those trees opposite, he felt he could breathe again without the air getting trapped in his throat. The journey across the hills and to the pass, and Switzerland seemed so close and there appeared to be quite a few places of cover. He sensed his wife was almost reluctant to leave the shelter of the forest.

Gravely they handed back to Teresa the crucifix the icons of Christianity that had been loaned them for this hazardous journey and Karl ripped from their coats the arm bands depicting the dreaded swastika.

'We'll not need those anymore. Esther, I'll take David. We must go. Now.'

He grabbed his son, almost knocking Teresa off her feet still holding the boys hand. The girl had got them this far, but they had to move.

Now.

Esther bent down until she was at the level to look in Teresa's eyes. There were tears in the girl's eyes and she was unsure whether her husband's roughness had caused them or was it she was already missing her new friend, or frightened at being left alone and having to find her way home.

'*Leibchen*. We have to go. You must get back to your *mutter* as fast as you can. You know the way back?'

Teresa's bottom lips quivered and she nodded.

Esther hesitated. What could she do? Esther hated leaving her alone.

'Will I see David again?' Teresa asked watching Karl, with David in his arms moving cautiously towards the edge of the flat land, looking back at Esther with impatience suddenly sharp on his face.

Esther couldn't bear it. She was such a little figure and the woman pulled her to her and hugged her tight.

'Of course. Of course,' she didn't believe that and she doubted the girl did either.

'You have been a very brave little girl. Thank you Teresa. But now we must go and you must go home.'

She let her go, straightened up and turned the child to face again the forest.

Esther Szabó gave her a gentle encouraging push. 'Go *leibchen* and God will protect you.'

With dragging feet Teresa walked a short distance between the initially sparse covering of trees, then turned round just the once. Already the family had raced across the open ground and disappeared into the shadows and thick undergrowth of the wood opposite. She sighed deeply causing her shoulders to rise above her ears, then finally turned back facing the way home.

The day was only partially warmed by the low, weakening autumn sun, now reaching the zenith for the time of the year. The old lady rubbed the knuckles on her right hand. The arthritic pain was always worse in the cold.
David.
Although over seventy years had passed since then she had a clear imagine of his quite long black curly hair, his eyes deep, dark and very round in his small, white pinched face.
Teresa had a clearer picture in her mind of that long ago child than of her own sweet daughter Emily who'd died of polio fifty three years before and her kind, gentle husband Ernest. She fingered her mother's crucifix she always wore round her neck, alongside the silver locket holding the photographs of her child and her man. He had given her the locket just after their daughter's birth. Often now she needed these to remember.
Had David and his parents managed to escape to Switzerland? She never knew the answer, but even now she hoped her little friend had gone on to live a full and happy life in his new home.

Teresa knew the way back home.

Even though it was now quite dark in the forest and there were noise all around, some strange and alarming as the nocturnal animals seemed to wake up to hunt, she knew the way and wasn't frightened.

She ran through the trees her instincts showing her the natural paths and ways. She ran so fast that sometimes it seemed her legs wouldn't move fast enough for her body and the momentum made her fall, or she tripped over a hidden branch. Once the little girl fell forward into a prickly bush that scratched her face and ripped her shawl, but undeterred Teresa picked herself up and brushed down the front of her coat. Somewhere she'd lost one of her mittens, but she'd kept tight hold of the now empty basket. Should she stop and pick a few mushrooms for her mother? Maybe not. All she really wanted was to get home, and warm herself in front of the fire and drink a mug of fresh warm goat's milk.

She ran through the trees, over the crushed bracken and undergrowth, startling a family of rodents foraging in the bushes. She ran across the clearing, where Franz from Berlin and the other soldier had poked the loose ground and mounds of dead leaves with the knives on their rifles, where David and his parents had hid. She slowed slightly just in case the soldiers had returned and would be very angry she had down as they'd told her. Would they take her away 'for questioning' like Gunter Mueller had told her they did with people who disobeyed their orders?

But the place was empty except for a small deer that had found her spilt mushrooms and soft berries from earlier. The animal raised its head and stood only for a second to stare, before disappearing into the trees.

Hilde Gőetschl had no real idea of how long she'd sat on the hillock. Time seemed to stand still although it had to be early evening, for the sun had all but disappeared behind the tops of the pines. Soon Josef and Leisl would be coming home expecting a nourishing meal after their day spent at the Schultz's. So much had happened since they left that morning that it felt like it was days ago. But she did not let her thoughts linger on Josef's reaction if she wasn't there waiting for their return with sizzling food in the pan and fresh bread from the oven. But they would be safe. However hungry, however tired, her husband and youngest child would be safe. All her being was focused on Teresa until her muscles, limbs and joints ached with the tension and her head throbbed, her eyes stung with the amount of unshed tears of grief at the growing possibility her daughter was dead or dying, alone in the forest. Her first born, often willful, clever and sweet natured, and no one knew better than Hilde, just how headstrong Teresa could be. She fought the image that would not leave her mind of the small, pathetic figure lying alone and lost in the cold and dark. If she let in the thoughts that the forest creatures would find her body and ---. No. No. Hilde shook her head fiercely from side to side. She would have to know the fate of Teresa or she would slowly go mad.

Standing on legs that threatened to collapse under her, the woman slowly started towards the gap between the trees, a natural opening into the forest. She suddenly stopped and swayed as a mix of nausea and dizziness overcame her.

At first it was only a flash of movement, then the sound of dried, fallen branches being snapped underfoot and the small figure of her daughter appeared. She looked very small, dwarfed to a slight body beneath the towering trees. She'd obviously been running, because she now stopped and out of breathe leant against one of the solid trunks until she could felt she could go further.

Hilde let out a cry, 'Teresa.' She ran towards her daughter, oblivious of the stream of tears down her cheeks. For the first time Teresa dropped the basket and ran as fast as her legs would carry her.

Mother and daughter met, Hilde lifting the child off the ground and hugging her until Teresa struggled. Hilde couldn't stop the sobs and tears of relief and Teresa matched the sentiment.

They stood and cried, and then she first shook the child angrily before hugging her so tightly Teresa thought she would break in two. Her mother hugged her with joy and relief until finally Hilde set her daughter back on her feet.

'You bad girl,' she scolded between strained bouts of sobs. 'I could slap you hard for going off like that. Anything could have happened to you.' Then hugged her again as if she'd never let go.

'What were they thinking of, putting my daughter in such danger?' she muttered under her breath, angry with the refugees.

Teresa was crying as if she'd never stop. Hilde calmer now, wiped her daughter's dirty face of tears and dirt.

'It's all right. You are safe.'

Her daughter seemed so distraught, so much crying it would make her ill. The shock must have affected her and Hilde was worried, she needed to get her daughter home and into the warmth and she was probably hungry too. A big bowl of broth and warm milk would make her feel much better.

'Teresa, *mien leibchen.* It's all right,' she spoke quietly and her arms went again round her daughter's slight shoulders.

'It's all right,' she affirmed. 'You are safe. David is safe now, so why do you cry so, child?'

Hilde was suddenly concerned. 'Are you hurt? Have you hurt yourself? She scrutinized her daughter's face and felt her limbs through her clothes. She'd been so pleased and relieved to see her run from between the closely packed trees that she'd not consider she might be hurt.

Through increasingly loud sobs, Teresa sniffed and muttered something.

'What is it? Where is the pain? Is it your belly?'

Teresa shook her head and stumbling over the words, tears tumbled from her eyes and nose, and dribbled flowed out of her open mouth.

'Tell me. Did the Szabo's do something to make you cry?'

'No *Mutti.*' Teresa struggled to stop crying, and sobbed and sniffed as she explained.

'Franz from Berlin and another soldier were in the forest with rifles and they were poking the ground with knives, just were David was hiding under some leaves. I was so scared I thought they were going to hurt David----.'

Oh no. Her young daughter had witnessed more than any child should. They'd killed the boy ---.

'Was David ---?'

'*Nein Mutti*. But I was so frightened that I wet my knickers.'

It was nearly dark when Josef and Leisl arrived home and by then Hilde had had time to wash and feed her daughter, who was no worse off for her adventure.

'Now remember, you promised not to tell anyone about the Szabós.'

Teresa seated at the table, clean and dressed in her bright pink and blue pinafore, dipping chunks of bread into the broth, nodded.

'Teresa. I mean it. You must never ever tell anyone about the family staying here and then you taking them through the forest.'

How could she be so sure? She was only seven and seven year old were too young to understand the full implications if the secret came out. Before Josef arrived she had to drill it into the child.

'You have promised not to tell on the Bible and holding your Rosary, you know what would happen if you broke that promise? Jesus would never be able to forgive you and you would go to Hell.'

What was she doing, filling her daughter's head with such threats? But she was so worried. It was better Teresa was in fear of the Devil himself than the risk of the whole family being arrested and shot, or transported to Mauthausen, the camp her husband had often excitedly talked about, just for helping those Jewish people.

With her elbow on the table top and her head resting wearily on her hand, Teresa sighed. Why did *Mutti* have to go on and on? She was so tired and her eyes kept closing.

98

'I know *Mutti*. I promised.'

Hilde had to be satisfied with that. It was quite a burden to rest on someone so young.

For days even weeks after the event, she worried and fretted over what might happen, but as the weeks went by and no army of soldiers banged on her door to take them away, she began to relax again. Had Teresa forgotten the incident? Hopefully it was fading as more recent items of interest filled her young life. Maybe it had become no more than a dream? It was never spoken off between mother and daughter again.

Chapter 10

The winter that year was long and bitter, with snow drifts banked up for weeks against their door so the girls were unable to go to school on the days it was very bad, even with their pairs of skis made for them by their father.

Josef had weeks of illness: having to spend most of his time in bed. Unable to get out and meet with his party friends he grew restless and short tempered concentrating only on his own self pity and interest and dismissive of his wife's quiet spells of anxiety and by January Hilde was sure of the worrying truth. She was pregnant.

The first and second missed period she put down to the trauma over the hiding then flight of the refugees coupled with the terrible fright that her daughter was dead, but by the new year and heaving bouts of morning sickness, she knew. Another pregnancy, even though she'd had two previous miscarriages and neither Teresa or Leisl's births had been easy, she knew Josef would be pleased, especially if this time it was his much wanted son.

She delayed telling him as long as possible. How could she know? What if he suspected? She struggled to remember dates during that crucial month of November. Was it Josef's, or Mueller's, baby?

Eventually though she had to say something to her husband. Her waist was thicken and she was increasingly tired and worn out after tending their small ménage of animals, the winter vegetable growing alongside the chalet wall, cooking, cleaning looking after the family needs and still taking in the townspeople stitching and mending.

Of course Teresa did what she could when not attending school of Mass as mother and daughter's did whenever the snow allowed them to get beyond the high drifts that seemed to cut off the farmstead from the rest of the town at least four or five times every winter.

Josef took her into his arms and kissed her. 'That is wonderful news. This time it will be a boy. I just know it will be a son and we will call him Josef after his father.'

He was overjoyed as she knew he would be quite oblivious to her own misgivings and the sudden wave of weariness that overwhelmed her. She felt faint with the worry. If only she could confide in Father Dominic, but even the hint that she had sinned and broken her marriage vows and he would excommunicate her forever. She would be forced to spend eternity in the fires of hell, And what of the child? If it wasn't her husband's would its fate be the same as hers? She worried day and night over this, uncertain and knowing that she could never confess to the priest and hope that God would forgive them both. More and more as the weeks went by she worried more, making her heart flutter in her chest and dizziness that made her clutch at any piece of furniture close enough for support until the feeling passed. The notion that she should confide in Heinrich Mueller over her doubts, didn't enter her head. In fact apart from his wife calling before Christmas with demands for a new outfit in time for the parties and festivities she would inevitable be attending with her important husband, Hilde only saw the man once when she returned to their big house next door to the *Rathaus* and he ignored her as if she was a mere servant.

If the fact his wife was very pale and quiet for most of the time ever concerned Josef then he chose to ignore it. She was pregnant and in his view for nine months these ailments were only to be expected.

Leisl chatted nonstop about a possible brother, and was very impatient at the wait. Teresa was more circumspect. A brother would be nice, but she knew it took many months before he would be born, but she'd already decided in her own mind they had to call him David.

Two things occurred within days of one another.

It was early March, and although the tops of the distance mountains and the hills held onto the snow, in the valley's spring had arrived in the guise of early spring flowers and the sounds of birds and insects. The air was crisp and fresh, and the whole of the Tyrol woke to breath in the new season.

As usual Teresa, Leisl and Hilde attended early morning mass in the small church, before they parted to go to the school house and Hilde walked slowly back home to start on more delicate hand stitching and embroidering on a Communion dress and veil for the Lehmann's daughter Maria.

She hoped Josef would have taken the chance in this warmer weather to get out and perhaps visit, his friends. He'd been so full of enthusiasm and wanting to join in the celebrations with the mayor, and Oberführer Schmit after hearing the victorious fall of Stalingrad in January. His recurring bronchitis meant he'd had to forgo that particular excitement, but at the opportunity he would don his thick coat and muffler, pull the armband over the sleeve and almost march in triumph the short distance to the tavern in the town.

Hilde was thankful for the break in the weather and a chance to walk slowly back home. She needed to think, not that thinking would give her answers or put things right again. She stumbled and almost fell, as her constant tiredness and worry pressed down on her shoulders. Although little more than four months pregnant, the child felt heavy and uncomfortable, but she knew she mustn't feel this way about an innocent child. Hilde couldn't help the resentment that bubbled in her throat and the alarming fluttering of her heart, and wondered if the child sensed this as it pushed against her ribs making her feel nauseous. What if it was Henrich Mueller? She knew that she'd know after its birth, but importantly would it have any of the mayor's characteristics so Josef would guess the truth of its conception?

The sun, still low in the sky, felt warm on her back and the scent of early thyme and the woody aroma of moss and lichen did nothing to lift her spirits.

Suddenly, unwelcome. Into the old woman's memory slipped a long forgotten image. Around her people, couples some with children passed by her bench with hardly a glance at Teresa and her bags of shopping. In her mind she was recalling times long ago.

Fraülein Gerda Weisz the teacher who had taken over after the strange disappearance of Herr Grassinger and his elderly widowed mother. She disliked her from the start and it was evident that the teacher had not liked Teresa. As clear as if she was standing before her now, she could see her tall, straight very thin body always wearing the same muddy grey skirt and jacket, thick Lyle stocking and utilitarian shoes, had the ability to push her head forward so her bony nose, small piercing colourless eyes and a lipless mouth that continually pinched was a symbol of never-ending disapprovement, without relaxing her ramrod stance. Her feet were large and her hands, thin with extraordinary long fingers, were the most memorable and the way she could whip the cane across the air until it sang, and landed on some poor unfortunate pupil's knuckles leaving pain and angry red wheals. Fraülein Weisz took almost fanatical delight in inflicting punishment for the very smallest of misdemeanors, almost to the same extend she had her school marching.

Marching, hands swinging, in time.

Left, right, left, right.

Hour after hour and for the glorious Third Reich.

Teresa knew she should take more interest in the teacher's lectures about the Thousand Year's Reign, and the hours of drilling into the impressionable young minds the wonders of Adolf Hitler. But the young girl soon grew bored and found gazing out through the window at the mountains in the far distance, and the rolling hills straddled with woods and pine forests in the middle distance, or the army trucks that often rolled passed the door, more of interest. She really would have rather have read one of the books, maps of the world and story books that use to sit on the shelves behind the teacher's desk, but now only held booklets and leaflets extolling the Nazi propaganda.

Teresa Hunt tried to shift her memory away from those times so long ago. She had been happy here in England with many wonderful times, but why should she remember so vividly, a time that was harsh and cruel?

Chapter 11

Most of the walk back to the chalet was uneventful for Hilde. It was only a short distance from the church home, but her feet seemed to drag today as if the sheer weight of her growing problem would drive her into the still frozen ground. So immersed in her own thoughts, she hadn't realized she had company until a voice at her side made her jump.

'Good morning Hilde.'

It was Lotti Hofler. Her daughter and Teresa were friends, but although the same age and had attended school at the same time, the lives of the two women were complete different. Lotti had always appeared slightly aloof as if the wife of a successful bank manager was far superior to a mere seamstress, although as with most of the town's women, she wasn't averse to calling on Hilde if she needed professional handmade clothes or repairs. It was odd that she was now at her side as if she'd purposely engineered this unusual meeting as it was far from a common occurrence, It made Hilde, her nerves already at breaking point, almost paranoid. What was Lotti Hofler after? What did she know or guess, and how many of her secrets would be gossiped over by the other wives and women? Or was she imagining things that didn't exist, and it was just two mothers strolling on a bright fresh morning exchanging chat about their daughters?

'Are you well, Hilde? You seem a little peaky, if I may say so.'

The small, plump woman, her yellow hair loose to her shoulders and frizzy from too much perming lotion, her face rosy-cheeked and eyes the deep blue of the sky fell in step beside the other. She wore the coat Hilde had made in the fall, the heavy woolen material in a shade of mustard that Teresa thought unbecoming of her bucolic, ruddiness.

'I'm well, thank you, but it has been a hard winter. How are you and Felix? Ingrid told my Teresa you have been suffering with your legs again.'

It was known by many that Lotti Hofler was a martyr to varicose veins that often laid her low for days at a time.

She glanced down at her feet encased in the fine leather boots.

'Ah well. We do what we can,' she said with a stoic sigh. 'I was warned by the doctors after I had Ingrid, the pregnancy and she was such a large size, she had caused irreparable damage to the veins in my legs. I am afraid I will suffer all my life. Sometimes they are swollen to the size of Bernhard Schults prize marrows.'

Hilde did her best to empathize but she was tired and longed to get home and rest her own legs.

Frau Hofler suddenly stopped and did a very strange thing. She grabbed Hilde's arm and glanced right and left as if expecting to be seen or overheard.

They continued on side by side, not speaking along the rough path winding between overgrown bushes, now acid green with new growth and the hint of buds about to open. Past scrubland bursting into new life with the misty cream and yellow heads of bracken and beyond gently rising to undulating meadows and hills with thick layers of early cornflowers, the richer blue of gentian, pure white oxeye daisies and clumps of primroses, scattered beneath scented broom. Even from this distance Hilde could see the outline of her home with the welcoming spiral of blue, grey smoke rising from its single chimney.

Of course there was no other person in sight. Their only company was the sheep no more than tiny dots on the horizon, the goats nimble footed scrambling over moss covered rocks and the occasional hawk seeking a tasty meal on the ground. The sounds were of cow bells and insects waking from their winter's sleep and already seeking out nectar from any obliging spring flower, and as a complete contrast to the country sounds, a distance barrage of gunfire coming from the general direction of the army barracks.

'What is it?' Hilde faced the other her eyes narrowed with concern. Was she feeling bad, a sudden attack of throbbing pains in her swollen legs?

'There is something I need to discuss with you,' Lotti had even lowered her voice, although it was hardly necessary.

'I --- we know what you did last year.'

Hilde felt faint and if it hadn't been for the arm still holding her own, she was sure she would have collapsed in a heap at the feet of this woman.

She knew. Oh dear God, Holy Mother. Jesus how did she know? How could she possibly know about Mueller and that she could possibly be pregnant by him?

'Hilde,' Lotti looked worried and held tighter as if sensing it was only her strength that was keeping the other from falling. 'It's all right. Only Felix and myself, know the truth. We, of course, will not repeat it to anyone else or if it got to the ears of that pompous Henrich Mueller or his friend Oberführer Schmit or the Nazi SS, we would all be in grave trouble.'

Hilde was finding it hard to speak. Her first assumption had been wrong, but now this woman was speaking of something else, and she didn't want to put her dread into words. In saving the refugees she had known she would be classed as a traitor, not only by the Germans, but the town and ultimately her own husband, but worse than that she had implicated her own daughter: an innocent seven year old. What would they do not just to her, but Teresa and even Leisl and Josef if and when this all came out? Could she plead, beg at least for the lives of her family, and ask Lotti to spare them? Closing her eyes against the terrible future, all her thoughts and anxieties tumbled in seconds through her mind and bending forward she heaved on a stomach empty of food.

'Hilde. Oh my dear,' she felt the cool hand of Lotti wiping her brow and opening her own she looked into troubled blue eyes.

'I can't imagine how strong and brave you must have been.'

'I don't know what you are talking about.' Hilde's mouth and throat were dry and she was finding it hard to swallow as acid bile rose in her throat. Had Teresa, after all the times she made her promise, told her friend Ingrid who then told the secret to her parents.

The old woman shifted on the bench. She was getting stiff and the wind that had been little more than a breeze a few hours ago was strengthening. A sudden gust sent a flutter of dead leaves from the branches of the sycamore and settled on the grass. Soon she told herself, she would have to go and get the shopping for her neighbour. Ms Gloria Riley. For some reason she needed the food urgently, but Teresa couldn't remember why. Lines of worry covered her forehead. She could remember what her neighbour had instructed her to buy and she would get so shirty, *a lovely word* shirty, *if she'd forgotten anything. She never had told not even Ernest after they married. She'd promised Mutti and Jesus, and she'd kept that promise. She shifty again, her old bones objecting to the solidness of the wood. No she'd never told.*

A large leaf, brown and crisp floated elegantly down and landed on one of the three the bulging plastic bags spread out on the ground at her feet. Teresa looked both confused and disturbed. When had she bought those things? Or was someone playing games with her tired mind?

'I'm talking about the Szabó family and how you took them in, fed and clothed them then helped them escape across the border into Switzerland.'

The dizziness returned. If only she had the energy to contradict or at least run, run far away from this woman, who she'd never really liked in the first place.

'Listen to me Hilde,' she was sounding very serious, the words hardly more than a forced whisper. 'You saved those people.'

Hilde took a couple of steps away but Lotti quickly grabbed her arms supporting the swaying woman.

'Over there,' she indicated a group of rocks forming a natural outcrop and green with moss and lichen. 'Let's rest and talk.'

She helped the stumbling, scared woman from the path to the smooth surface rocks and neither spoke again until they were seated and Lotti was thankful to see some colour returning to the other's cheeks. She still thought she looked too pale and even just holding her upper arm for support, Hilde Góetsch had seemed little more than skin and bone. She wondered if the woman was sickening for something, but didn't say having something of great importance that needed to be said.

'I have to tell you something that will help you understand, Hilde,' the plump little woman began, her focus on the hills in the middle distance and the towering snow-capped mountains beyond. Her family was very patriotic, and loved this land of natural beauty.

'You probably don't know because of his fair colouring, but Felix is Jewish.' Hilde, who had been sitting fidgeting and fretting, and wanting more than anything to jump up, run home and slam and shuttered the door against all the worries and terrors that were happening beyond her own safe world, now blinked hard and turned to face Lotti with surprise etched in her eyes.

How could that be?

Felix Hofler was a tall, ramrod straight well-built man who always dressed elegant and smart as befits an important banker in the most prestigious bank. He had thick

111

wavy hair and his bushy eyebrows were so blonde as to be almost white. He was a person who had very little humour in him, and appeared aloof and distant to anyone except his close family and few friends. He was someone she'd known all her life and as a boy then man he had always been the same.

'His ancestors came from Hungary, white Jews and over the ages married Gentiles like me. But secretly he always remained true to his creed if not the religion. I don't think anyone even suspected as he was brought up as a Christian and we married in a catholic church. Ingrid doesn't know and with the situation as it is in Austria, we think it best to keep it so.'

Her face softened and a small line of concern formed between her brows. She sounded almost childlike when she pleaded earnestly, 'You'll keep our secret, please Hilde?'

So now both shared life-threatening secrets and needed the other.

'Of course I will.'

'You'll not tell Josef?'

No. Definitely not her husband.

How had it come to this that she had to keep secrets from her own man? They had always shared everything from the day of their marriage, only circumstances of the war and how it was splitting ideology and families had changed that.

'No. Not Josef.' Hilde knew better than anyone just how much her man had been seduced into the brutality of Fascism.

But something didn't seem right.

'But your husband is a member of the Party. Like Josef he attend all the meetings and is a confidante of Oberführer Schmit.'

Lotti Holfer nodded and gazed again out onto the land of her birth.

'He is in the best position, with his status in the town, to gather information to pass on to the Allies.'

'A spy?'

'If you like. He and I do not like what the German's have done to our country, aligning us up with them and alienating Austria with the rest of the world. He especially hates what they are doing to the Jews. Whatever propaganda has been handed to people like your husband, the Nazi's have set up death camps and are slaughtering all Jews in an attempt at genocide.'

'Perhaps Josef doesn't know this. Perhaps I should tell him the truth ---.' Because the truth she knew this to be, no matter how much Josef had proclaimed otherwise.

Lotti looked horrified.

'No. No. No one must ever know or we will be betrayed and suffer the consequences. Please Hilde.'

For a few minutes they sat silent, each deep in their own thoughts. The sun was warming, and a formation of aircrafts droning overhead was the only sound to disturb the stillness.

'Why have you told me this, Lotti?'

'I have told you so much, so it can do no more harm to tell you the rest. Our lives are in your hands now. Two years ago, Felix and others started an underground movement to try and move as many of Hungarian Jews out of Austria as they could. It has been successful in getting men and women, whole families into neighbouring safe countries, by train, disguised trucks and even small planes and under the very noses of the German army and men like Oberfrüher Schmit. He is a cruel, sadistic man by all accounts,'

Oh God, thought Hilde, Josef, my own husband classes that man as a good friend. She stayed silent as Lotti continued.

'Felix knew nothing of the flight of the Szabós until he was contacted by banker friends in Switzerland, who told him about your role in their escape. It was truly amazing and they are now safe and very grateful to you and Teresa.'

Hilde was glad to hear they were safe, but in her mind she wanted to forget all about the episode and concentrate on her own life and in particular her dilemma. The world might be at war, with neighbour fighting neighbour, but she had her own hell to deal with.

Lotti Holfer took a deep breath before continuing. It all rested on how Hilde would react after she was asked.

'We ---- Felix need you to do it again.'

'What?' Hilde was alarmed.

'A family has managed to get as far as Salzburg. They've had help so far from across the Hungarian border and in a few days, will be brought in the back of a truck transporting sheep to a place east of the town. It's important they get across the border into Switzerland as soon as possible.'

'Who are they?'

'Who they are doesn't matter. What matters is that they need help to get to safety. If the Nazi's get wind of this there will be a wide scale manhunt.'

Hilde knew what she was asking although it hadn't yet been put into words. She wanted none of it. The last time she'd had no choice but to hide them and get them to safety, but now she had. She was not about to put her own family in danger. How could this woman and her husband expect it of her?

'No,' she said emphatically a sudden unexpected fluttering of her heart making her clasp her chest.

'All we ask is that they be brought to your barn under the cover of darkness the day after tomorrow. It can be arranged so Josef is having beer with Felix so he'll not know anything. If you could provide food and water for twenty four hours, nobody'll know they are in your barn. On the tenth again Felix will suggest a night of cards with some friends and include your husband again. He'll come to your house for Josef and drive him to our house and back again later. While he keeps Josef busy it will give you the

114

opportunity and time to do, as Teresa did before, and lead them through the forest to the same place, and to the hidden pass into Switzerland. --- How it is the German's haven't discovered it yet is a miracle.'

Hilde raised her voice, sending a startled bird skywards.

'No I won't do it. How can you ask me?'

Her heart had started to thump in her throat and she was experiencing the same nausea she had felt earlier. She stood from the rock and felt immediately dizzy. Lotti stood and again held her arm to steady her.

'There is no alternative. These people are in real danger and if caught will not survive for long. You are their only way to safety, Hilde.'

'But I cannot put my family in danger. Not again.'

'They will be safe. I swear. Felix has everything in place and it has been carefully planned to the last.'

After more persuading, Hilde eventually agreed.

'But Lotti this has to be the last time.'

'Of course,' nodded the banker's wife.

Chapter 12

The second event was unexpected and tinged with sadness. This happened only hours after her unwelcomed guests arrived at her barn and were safely hidden in the hay loft.

As if part of Felix's fool-proof plan it was a inky black, starless night the moons face hidden from sight by a thick layer of clouds.

Hilde miscarried.

The pregnancy so far had not gone well. She was now in her fourteenth week, but this was only a guess. So far she hadn't called on the doctor to confirm the dates, although knowing the bad times she'd had with her previous pregnancies he would be far from pleased she'd left it so long. She felt so ill. Her head ached and her heart raced alarmingly, and she was losing weight, weight she could hardly afford to lose. Her anxiety only made matters worse as she tossed and turned each night beside her deeply sleeping, contented husband, and picked uninterested at her food. Josef, so wrapped up in the Party and how the mighty German army and the powerful Axis was defeating the enemy: bragging almost daily in the way of Hitler's Anti-Semitic ravings and in the name of the Reich how Jews, the deformed and abnormal, gypsies and any others they thought as undesirables were being systematically intimidated, humiliated, tormented and beaten by mob rule in a lot of the cities. Hilde listened and was inwardly ashamed of her husband, who had been drawn into this hysterical propaganda, and cruel ideology, but kept silent. Her thoughts, her worries were her own. If he noticed her appearance then his new found fanaticism blinded him to his wife's fragile condition. She loved him as much as the day they'd married, he was the father of her girls, but he was a Josef she didn't understand anymore. Occasionally he would gently stroke her rounded stomach and his eyes would soften at the thought of a son.

The pain in her back had increased throughout the day and Hilde struggled with her usual work around the house, the amount of sewing she had to do, and the planting in their small vegetable garden the early summer crop. She thought she needed something to keep her mind off the coming night. She prayed and prayed first at early morning Mass then under her breath during the following hours that she'd not have to do this. She hoped Felix Hofler had another better plan to get these refugees to safety by other means, hidden in a truck, in a goods train or as he'd done with others, a small light airplane. Anything was preferable to relying on her, and potentially putting her family at risk. As the hours drew on and she made their evening meals as usual, her husband dressed in his Sunday suit for his evening with his friends and Teresa and Leisl played and squabbled as usual, and Hilde grew ever more anxious until she felt her head would burst and her back would break.

With her husband out and her daughters in bed under the roof, she sat nervously waiting. She clasped and unclasped her hands, stood to ease her back and sat again, until at nine o'clock she heard the engine as the truck drew up outside her house.

She hurried outside, oblivious to the cold that had settled on the night and was attacking her face and hands. The driver was a stranger he gave Hilde only a cursory nod after climbing from the cab and running round to release the backboard. He drew alongside the barn's double doors so Hilde pulled them open and waited, fighting down a sudden rush of bile in her throat.

A man jumped down, followed by another, the two then helped down the older woman and finally the three

118

turned their attention to the final person, a young man or boy who struggled to alight the short distance to the dusty earth.

It was happening so fast, as if practiced with precision, as the four ran inside the barn, the driver ran back to the cab and drove away at speed.

All this without a word having been spoken.

Hilde followed them inside the barn as the men pulled the doors close behind her. The old woman and the boy had already made their way to the ladder to the hayloft and with difficulty were climbing into the relative warmth of the scattered straw. The men stood and watched as if making sure they were safe before one spoke to Hilde.

'My name is Manfred and this is Lukós. The woman is Brigitta and the young man, her son is Viktor. You do not need to know more for your own safety,' his speech was clipped and spare.

'The plan is to continue as arranged. We stay here until the tenth and once dark, you will be given the time on the day. Then you will guide us to the pass that will take us to the Swiss border. I have been told only you know the way through that forest.'

He paused and glanced towards the loft.

'Brigitta and Viktor have had a long, hard day and I would be grateful if you could provide us with food and drink, before we try to settle down for the night.'

It was said without emotion and the other man didn't say a word, except it was evident that his thoughts and concern were with the woman and boy who had climbed out of sight. The cluster of hens and the inquisitive goat's whose home had been invaded, were ignored.

After she'd done their bidding, including bringing extra blankets for the cold night, Hilde left them to it, making sure the barn was bolted. On returning with the requested hot food she had handed it to the same man who had given her a small bow and a courteous thank you, but of the other three there was no sign. It had been a hard journey for them and Hilde guessed they were worn out and needed rest before the next hazardous part.

The pain in her back and across her lower stomach was getting worse as she stood alone in the large room of the chalet. Outside the night was cold and dark, and a sudden sharp pain bent her double and she clutched at the edge of the table for support, and the innocent, unborn child she had regretted, resented and in her darkest moments despised and felt overwhelming guilt for what could have been an abusive conception, was no more.

It was a long night, full of pain and Hilde wasn't fully conscious of the doctor coming and sadly shaking his head, or the whispered conversation between Dr. Brunner and Josef.

In the odd moment of consciousness, Hilde thought she heard the doctor say, 'Hilde has lost a lot of blood,' and 'No more children, Josef. Her heart is not strong for another pregnancy.'

Then Hilde slipped again into the quiet, welcomed and healing sleep.

The next morning it was a surprise to Josef that Lotti Hofler arrived early, driving her husband's Daimler. She bustled about, as usual, organizing the girl's breakfast and sending them off to school. He was in the way, as she, unexpectedly, nursed and fussed around his wife who had been told to stay in bed for at least a week.

He was relieved to get out and stroll into the town, convinced he'd be leaving his wife in good hands. He was sad, and angry that he would have a son after all. He knew it was unreasonable to blame Hilde, but why had she not seen Doctor Brunner after she had all the trouble having Leisl. Her selfishness meant he would never have a son now and he was thankful to be able to get out of the house and her presence for a few hours.

'Why didn't you tell me you were pregnant,' demanded Lotti as she savagely tucked the covers around Hilde and made an effort to plump the pillow. The anger in her words revealed her real worry.

'We wouldn't have expected you to take such a risk in your condition,' she couldn't hide her irritation as if Hilde had done this to scupper the well- made plans.

'This escape had been weeks in the planning and now it could all end in disaster.

Hilde sighed and fought back the tears that seemed so easy. She felt, bruised and battered, a sense of loss and guilt, and the last thing she needed was to be made to feel even worse than she did. She never asked to get involved. The people in the barn meant nothing to her, and at that moment she didn't care about their fate. All she wanted was to be left alone and sleep.

'It's too late now to make other arrangements for tomorrow's night, and you'll be in no state to guide them through the forest. I suppose we could just give Manfred a rough map through the forest --.'

Hilde, who had spent her live living beside the forest that stretched further than the eye could see, knew it wasn't possible for strangers to find their way through to the opposite side, never mind being able to locate the actual opening that led to the pass. This narrow pass between the hills and mountains was invisible, unless one knew the precise place. 'That would be impossible. The forest is a living breathing organism, and constantly changing season on season. It's easy to become disorientated and one tree can look like another.'

Lotti glared at the woman's attempt at humour. This was deadly serious. She was losing her patience. This whole situation was becoming a nightmare.

'It's the only option left. There is so little time to make another plan. All this stress is not helping Felix with his blood pressure.'

Hilde was tired of having to feel apologetic and she wanted Lotti to go.

'After you give them food I want them out of my barn before my husband returns,' she sounded weepy and felt increasingly weary.

'We can't do anything that quickly, Hilde. Be reasonable. These are four lives we are talking about. Would your conscience let you live with the consequences?'

Hilde didn't answer, right then she didn't care, but lay back and closed her eyes.

Lotti was not to be beaten. She moved around the room, picking up a small carved animal on the mantle and a dish left on the dresser as if she'd not seen them before.

'Teresa could take them through the forest,' she suggested hesitantly, as if the thought had just popped into her head

Hilde opened her eyes with alarm. 'No.'

'Why not?' asked Lotti warming to the idea. 'The child has played all her live in the forest, and after the last time ---.'

'I did not want her to risk her life like that. What sort of a mother do you think I am? Teresa can be stubborn and she went into the forest with the family without me knowing. That was the first and last time and I'm not putting her in danger again.'

She tried, and hoped, to sound determined but her voice was little more than a weak croak.

'No. I'll not allow it. Would you let Ingrid put her life at risk?' she asked mother to mother.

Lotti Hofler didn't answer and Hilde turned onto her left so her back was to the woman, and closed her eyes.

Teresa and Leisl skipped then ran home from school. It had been a long day in which Fraülein Weisz had been extra ferocious in her demands for formation marching around the school yard.

'Keep in step. Swing your arms. I'll make you into fine specimens of Hitler Youth if it's the last thing I do.'

Round and round the yard. Hour after hour until many of the children were crying with exhaustion. All the time Teresa's thoughts were back home. Her mother was sick. She didn't know why, but Doctor Brunner had been to see her and she heard him say she had to stay in bed. *Mutti* never stayed in bed, like *Vater*. *Mutti* was never ill. But if doctor Brunner said she had to stay in bed for at least two days, then she had to be even more poorly than Teresa had been two winters ago, when she'd caught scarlet fever and had to live with the other sick children in that big hospital without ever seeing anyone except the stern faced nurses. She'd not liked that one bit, and had been glad when she was allowed home again.

Hilde wasn't going to have to stay at the big hospital in the town, but Teresa and Liesl had been instructed by their father that she needed rest and they had to keep quiet. It had been a long, worrisome day.

The little girl had no idea of the four in the barn as the sisters ran the last few yards in front of the bolted double doors, towards the chalet. The animals, usually housed in the barn, were running loose outside, but didn't cause concern as the girls scattered the hens and avoided the head-butting from Gertrude the large nanny goat.

Thankfully her mother was up and although even to the child she appeared pale, she was preparing the meal for when her father returned. It would be days before she explained to her daughters they would not be getting a baby brother or sister after all.

Chapter 13

It was the morning of the tenth. Teresa and Leisl went off to school, and Josef strolled down to the town. He needed to get out of the sudden claustrophobic feel of his home. He was still reeling from the loss of the baby, who could have been the son he wanted and unable to look his wife in the eye without feeling unreasonable resentment. Only Hilde knew the secret hiding in the barn so close to her family and the thought only heightened her depression. Tonight she would be rid of this worry.

With no interest and very little strength left she'd got up that morning to prepare breakfast and waved off the girl's and then Josef. If she noticed his quietness and coldness towards her, she hardly noticed. Once alone she took her unwanted guests food, not expecting and not receiving anything more than a nod and slight bow of thanks from the stern looking Manfred, and once again seeing nothing of the others as if the very presence of their current hostess, send them scurrying to the hidden corners of the hayloft. Hilde didn't care. She would be glad when the danger was passed and this episode was over.

She sat her head in her hands, feeling too weak to do more than let stress-filled thoughts play over and over in her mind.

She heard the sound of a car's engine and lifted her head to see the large imposing limo parked in front of the barn doors, scattering the hens in every direction and sending the gaggle of geese marching off to a safe corner of the yard.

Lotti Hofler stepped from the Daimler and furtively went through the doors into the gloomy barn. She was out again within a minute and walking towards the chalet door.

'How are you feeling, Hilde?' she asked, but it was a question born of necessity more than of concern.

'I'm all right,' Hilde answered rubbing a hand across her weary eyes.

'Good. Good. Now everything is to go ahead as planned. Elza Schultz has said she's only too pleased to help out in the circumstances: I told her about your miscarriage.'

Having her situation discussed by the other women in the town filled her with alarm and irritation, but she hadn't the energy to object. Lotti had always been a force to reckon with no matter who she offended, and especially if she had a pet project. Except this saw much more than organizing a fest or hosting a banker's dinner. Hilde sighed.

'Elza has agreed to have Leisl to stay tonight, she likes playing together with Corinna and Tomas. She wanted to have Teresa as well, but as we know that wouldn't have done at all, so I said you needed her to help around the place.'

Everything felt unconnected and her words floated in the stillness of the room. Outside the hens scratched and through the window she could see the goats climbing a nearby craggy rockery that sat alongside the steam. Its crystal-clear waters, fed from the fast thawing snow-capped mountains and hills, rushed over the shallow depths, sparkling in the sunlight.

'Felix has arranged another evening of cards, so Josef will be out of the way.'

Hilde wanted to argue, but knew it was hopeless. This was out of her hands now.

'If you could coach Teresa ---.'

'She not doing it,' Hilde's voice low and hoarse with emotion threatened to drown in tears of rage.

'Now come on. There is no alternative. Do you want to have the lives of these people on your conscience? You and Teresa will be saving them in the name of God.'

'Don't bring God's name into this mess. This war is down to human madness and now you want me to risk my daughter's live, again. She's seven.'

Lotti was growing flustered and knew she had to calm the woman. Hilde Gőetschl had been through a lot in the last few days, it was only natural she'd be emotional. But this situation was critical.

'I know, but she is brave ---.'

Hilde lifted her head and gazed at the woman seated opposite across the well-scrubbed table.

'Who are they?'

'I'm not sure I understand--.'

'Who are those four people so important you think it's all right to put my family at risk, just so they can escape across the border?'

'I don't think you need to know ---.'

'Lotti. Who are they?' she repeated, her voice growing stronger and louder. She fought back the fatigue and the sudden alarming thumping of her heart. Doctor Brunner had warned her against getting too upset.

Lotti Hofler sighed.

'The men were members of the Hungarian Second Army and now they are escorting the --- them to Switzerland.'

'Who?' Hilde wanted the truth.

Lotti sighed again resigned to the fact this weary young woman was not going to agree to anything unless she knew part of the truth at least.

'The old woman, Brigitta, is the maid servant to Hungarian aristocrat. The person disguised as a young man is a daughter of the family. Her parents tried to get away but were murdered, their property confiscated or destroyed and any servants that weren't killed captured and sent to camps in Germany. Only Brigitta and the girl got away and if she'd

127

remained in her native Hungary or even here in Austria for too long, she will be arrested and killed. That's all I'm saying --- and I've probably said more than I should.' A look of worry had clouded her usually rosy outlook.

The young man was a girl?

The room spun and Hilde thought she would faint. It all sounded like a fairy tale. Something from Grimm's Fairytales she would have read to her daughters. Beguiling, yet make-believe, of princesses in enchanted castles

'That's all you need to know,' Lotti was insisting. 'It's imperative they get across the border tonight.'

The old woman was feeling cold and her memories were fading into the murky past. How much had really happened, and how much was her mind paying tricks?

In the distance she heard the single bells sounding in a continual drone in the church close by.

Remembrance Day and fields of poppies.

All around the chalet, alongside the fast moving stream, in the crevices, nooks and crannies between the rocks grew the wild Alpines and there had been the carpets of flowers in swathes of rainbow hews that coloured her young world. A sudden overwhelming sense of homesickness, for a fast and a home she would never see again.

Teresa couldn't stop staring at the figure that stood before her. It was a boy, or at least she thought he was a boy, but the hat he wore the rim pulled down and covering his hair, did not hide the small nose, shapely mouth or weak chin. The jacket and trousers, although of good quality, hung on his slight frame as if made for someone much bigger. His skin was fine and unblemished, unlike the old woman, his mother, who was sharp eyed and wrinkled and fussed over him as if he was a baby. It seemed he couldn't even stand on his own without support, because the two men, Teresa was told were Manfred and Lukós continued to ask if he was all right with much bows and clicking of heels. All this made Teresa want to laugh, but *Mutti* had told her this was very serious and she must be a big girl and show them the way to the other side of the forest as quickly and as silently as she could. Just like the first time, but this time it would be in the dark.

This was exciting. An adventure.

'Now remember *leibchen*, the Baby Jesus will protect you from harm. This is our secret.'

It was another dark evening, the sun had long set and the clouds had settled low on the mountain tops and dipped down into valleys.

With only the minimum of words to his wife, Josef had changed and set out for his card game, Leisl was at the Schultzs, and only Teresa and her mother remained at home.

With hugs and warnings, and tears of dread freely falling, Hilde hugged her small daughter and then gave her a gentle shake.

In single file, Teresa quickly followed by the alert Manfred, then Brigitta, Viktor and Lukós at the rear, they moved swiftly first following the line of the stream down the contours of the gradually slopping valley beyond the ridge of trees atop the hill and towards the same natural rocks that formed a shelter and were previously Hilde had sat and waited for Teresa's return. This time she would be waiting in fear and dread back at the chalet. This time for her mother, time would stand still until she held her daughter in her arms once more.

Forty minutes later, moving as fast as they could, even though the old woman was out of breathe and it seemed more than one the boy looked like he might faint with exhaustion, they reached the first of the tall pine on the outskirts of the deep, thick forest. Only the two older men seemed able to keep going --- and Teresa who would have run and skipped ahead of them if Manfred hadn't stopped her.

'Stay close. We mustn't lose sight of one another,' he warned the child who reluctantly he'd been force to put his complete trust in.

They stopped while Brigitta and Viktor caught their breath, and Teresa would really have liked to ask them things, but Manfred and Lukós stood aside and whispered together, while the woman fussed over the boy as if he was poorly, just like David had been. Perhaps if she sang the same lullaby, but the boy didn't look like he would appreciate her attempt at trying to make him better. Teresa stayed quiet and waited, concentrating on kicking up a pile of dead leaves at her feet. Her mother had said she'd be tired and argued this with the man. But she wasn't. Not even a little bit.

After a while they set off again, now stepping deep into the forest that closed around them like a choking shroud. Even Teresa so use to the forest and its ways, having played amongst the trees all her life but never after sunset, found the night sounds intimidating. As they walked quickly but stealth fully into the blackness, there were the nighttime sound of small animals in the undergrowth, the hooting of an owl and the occasional larger animal blundering its way through shrubs and bushes. Insects, moths flitted by close enough to touch a face, a cheek or the threat of tangling its wings in hair. The two men Manfred and Lukós each had a torch that although, unable to penetrate the thickest density, helped to stop anyone from tripping over hidden roots or fallen branches.

The one, who seemed to be their main concern, was the boy. Teresa was unable to think of without an understandable feeling of distain. She stood silently apart from the party and waited, watching with little understanding, each time Viktor demanded they stop to rest. It was taking longer than was necessary but Teresa decided, the young man had to be sick, just like her father. He couldn't run or hurry either.

Teresa was eager to take then the route she'd known all her life, through the forest to the east that, providing she followed the same animal tracks and paths, and recognized certain clearings and natural landmarks would eventually bring them out at the part where the pines were growing sparse. Beyond the narrow area of scrub and overgrown grass, pointed the way to the small copse of trees to the left and the mountain pass to freedom.

Manfred in the lead, with Lukós taking the rear, kept their handguns at the ready in case of trouble. Teresa eyed the weapons held firm and pointing forward with caution and alarm, hoping they didn't suddenly fire them and frighten her. Perhaps she'd hum the lullaby to help her concentrate on this most important chore.

The humming helped her walk in step. Marching just like Fraülein Weisz had demanded of her.

Left, right. Swing those arms in time.

They stopped at the very clearing where David and his parents had hid covered in leaves when Franz from Berlin and the other soldier had poked and prodded the ground with those fierce looking knives. The forest was silent of everything except the natural sounds, and a break in the tree's branches they could just about see streaks of grey sky where the thick layer of cloud had parted. A sound, a crash of something or someone moving unhindered through the undergrowth started them. Manfred, always alert, gun ready, turned towards the sound while Lukós who'd been sitting on a rotting tree trunk stood and followed the leader, turning slowly on the balls of his feet, gun pointed and cocked ready for action. The old woman was breathing hard but stood close to the boy who was crying quietly. Teresa watched the group, quite unconcerned about the forest noises. She knew from the sound and the movement it was probably no more than a wild pig foraging with its long hairy snout, and also knowing that with their bad-tempered natures, it was best left well alone.

With the wisdom of a child and her knowledge of the trees and woods she slowly shook her head and crossed her arms, and waited impatiently.

'How far now, child?' asked Brigitta as another sound, a hooting owl this time made the youth cry out with alarm and fear.

'Just through there. Do you see between those trees over there?'

Lukós was nervous. 'Yes but when will we be out of this place. I don't like nature, never did.'

Manfred looked at the large watch on his wrist.

'We've been travelling for nearly an hour and a half. We need to be at the rendezvous by midnight.'

The boy known as Viktor spoke for one of the few times. His voice was high pitched and had not been the voice Teresa had expected. His voice seemed even higher than Gunter Mueller's.

'I'm tired. I can't go on.'

'You have to keep going,' coaxed Brigitta, his mother, with little conviction in her words.

Manfred having scouted a small area around the group, and sure they had only heard animals moving around, 'We have to move on.'

As before with Teresa and Manfred in the lead, they stepped out of the clearing and once more into the close knit trees their long straight trunks enclosing the five like a prison cell.

No one said a word as stumbling on unseen obstacles they continued on. They could see very little ahead and only the round spotlight arcs from the two powerful torches gave a certain feeling of security.

Where they going in the right direction? The men had no idea: both had lost any sense of directions. They could have been going round in circles and they were all at the mercy of this seven year old peasant girl. Manfred not known for his belief in a God now repeated the prayers he'd learnt from the Rabbi as a child.

They had resumed their journey and been travelling for another fifteen minutes when they heard the dogs.

Chapter 14

Hilde Gőetschl sat quietly and alone. It was almost unheard of that she would have the chalet to herself in the evenings, and for once she was thankful to be able to relax against the hard back of the settle and rest her eyes, without the need to stitch or sew a garment, or check on her daughters or the animals or her husband. Hilde was very worried. The last few days had been more than she could have coped with, the miscarriage, the refugees hiding in the barn and now her own seven year old daughter in mortal danger, and she felt helpless to do anything other than sit quietly and pray. God, Jesus the Holy Mother would look after Teresa and keep her safe. If only she'd been stronger, had not felt so weak she would not have agreed to any of this. All the pity in the world she had for the terrible plight of the Hungarian Jews would mean nothing if her daughter came to harm. She read the comforting passages from the Bible open on her lap and held the crucifix, suspended from a fine chain around her thin neck, so tight her fingers stiffened and the figure of Christ pressed into her palm.

A sound outside her door, and she woke from her fitful dozing, the heavy book slid to the floor from her knee. A car's engine. It was just after ten o'clock and the night was inky dark.

Moments later the car stopped the door opened and slammed disturbing the peace and a loud urgent knocking on her door, brought the woman to her weary feet.

'Hilde. Thank goodness. I thought I'd be too late to stop you.' Lotti Hofler rushed inside bringing with her the cooling air.

'They are still in your barn? Please tell me they are still hiding in your barn.'

Hilde didn't need to be hear more, she could see the anguish in the woman's face and hear it in her shaking voice. She felt for the arm of her husband's chair and sat down, her eyes on the her visitor's face. It revealed stark fear. Frau Hofler was so scared her deep blue eyes, usually calm, were now large and staring. Beads of sweat sat on her brow and a fine sheen covered her rosy cheeks. She licked her lips as if they were too cracked and dry to open.

'Lotti, tell me what's happened,' Hilde struggled to sound in control and fought down the rising hysteria that threatened to overtake her senses.

'We need to stop them from leaving,' Lotti was growing ever more agitated and paced the floor, wringing her hands in obvious despair. Her usually immaculate hairstyle was unkempt and her face powder, that she always bragged was the finest Helena Rubenstein's from Paris, France was patchy and smeared as if applied with little thought, but nevertheless a part of who she was, her full length fur coat was unfastened and on her feet she had a pair of shoes completely unsuitable for trailing across a farm yard but a testament to her present state of mind.

'Who from leaving?'Hilde was finding it hard to concentrate. She felt hot and a sudden dizziness made the floor tilt at her feet.

'The people in your hayloft. They can't leave tonight.'

'You're too late. They've gone, left over an hour ago ----.Why --?' She spotted the Bible fallen and left on the handmade rug, open at a page. She desperately wanted to reach down and pick it up, and lose herself in the wonderful words of comfort and wisdom. For the moment her limbs refused to do her bidding. Her heart was racing and her mouth felt dry so she couldn't add more to her unasked questions.

'I've had to leave Felix with his card game and rush over here as quick as I could when I heard ---.'

'Heard what ---?' Hilde wished her heart would slow down.

'They know something. The Nazi's know about our party making for the border.'

'How?'

Lotti continued her pacing the floor, the handwringing had given over to running her fingers through her hair and biting at her bottom lip.

'I don't know. Someone found out and reported their presence in the area, or someone talked. It's not impossible that sympathizers to the Party have been spying on the comings and goings. Felix has always been suspicious that people at the bank or even in his circle of friends would turn against him, if they could find a reason. Some are very jealous of his position and influence --.'

'You mean my daughter ---?' Hilde interrupted, not in the least interested in this woman's husband with his lofty status. She'd had little to do with the Hoflers apart from their daughter being Teresa's friend. Since Lotti Lunt had married the banker the woman moved in very different circles. 'Lotti,' she insisted a lump forming in her throat.

'Tell me what's happening?'

'I don't know, but it's probable the German are searching the woods and forest.'

Hilde let out a loud, animal wail. She couldn't stop it. It rose in pitch until she didn't even recognize her own sound. Lotti startled, then calmly ran to her and slapped her hard across the face. She gathered the weeping, now quieter woman in her arms. The fur of her coat was crushed and wet with the tears as she held her tight against her waist, until the tears eased.

'What can we do? Oh Mary, Mother of God, what can I do?

She couldn't take anymore. She felt her heart was breaking.

'They have Manfred and Lukós to protect them. Don't worry, they'll keep everyone safe.' The words seemed false and weak. Lotti Hofler couldn't think of anything else to say.

Manfred froze. Ever alert, his gun arm raised, the torch he lowered until the beam was hidden beneath his arm but just giving a halo of light for the others. They stood very still, and Lukós switched off his torch and moved to stand beside the leader.

The braying of the dogs, the number and distance unclear in the denseness of the trees, was to directly in front. If they kept going in the same direction there was no way to avoid the dogs and their handlers. Now the torchlight was dimmed it seemed to the child and the others the forest was alive with the hidden and unseen. She didn't like this new, very dark menacing forest. It was nothing like the friendly trees that stood tall and proud with the soft cushion underfoot and the wonderful pine and earthy scents, that she grown to love but she had only ever known in daylight.

'It could be hunters or poachers,' ventured Lukós trying to see beyond the trees to the right and seeing only blackness thick and threatening.

Manfred answered low and cautious. 'Could be, but we can't take any chances. We can't possibly expect to outrun the hounds if it's us they are looking for. Teresa stood uncertain what to do next. What would *Mutti* want her to do? She'd not told her what to do if they were being chased by dogs. Teresa was frightened of big dogs, and these sounded very big.

The youth was crying again as the old woman pulled at his arm encouraging him towards large overgrown bushes.

'Girl --,' he growled, bending to her height, Manfred roughly grabbed Teresa's shoulder making her squirm at the sudden harshness. '--- We can't go forward, is there another way to the pass?'

Teresa pulled herself free from his strong grip, and already her bottom lip trembled with uncertainty.

'I don't know.' She was indignant and bruised, but above all scared. They had ignored her up to then, only speaking in clipped sentences making sure she was leading in the right direction. Now this man was peering down at her with a hard, piercing glare. The others stared at them showing only the whites of their eyes, in blank, grey faces. They were watching her, waiting for answers.

'You have to know another way. Tell me,' his face was pushed so close to her own she could smell tobacco on his breath, just like her father. Except *Vater* was nice and made her feel safe, were as this man was stern and unfriendly.

'I don't know. I don't know,' her voice broke with a mixture of hurt and fear. Teresa felt so scared now. This man, this stranger and three more she strangers, made her very scared and she began to cry. Her eyes overflowed and her nose ran. Her mouth drooped open as she fought back the tears.

'I want *mein Mutti*. I want *mein Mutti*.' Teresa cried harder and louder, rising to a near scream, and effectively disturbing birds nesting high in the trees overhead. Lukós moved quickly to place a calloused hand across her mouth.

'Shut up.'

'Keep her quiet,' demanded an angry Manfred. The sound of the dogs was moving closer and he was sure he'd heard the snapping of branches and crunching of feet on the forest floor.

Bending again to the child's eye-line he looked into her terrified tear-streaked face. He needed to make her understand the severity of the situation without upsetting her anymore. He was meant to be the one protecting with all the answers and this child was probably their only way to freedom.

'Listen to me, *leibchen*,' he softened his voice to one of gentle persuasion. 'I know you're frightened, but your parents--- your *Mutti* would want you to be a brave little girl.'

He tried further soothing noises, then impatiently stood up and took a deep breath his mind working fast. For a moment the girl was sobbing quietly, but not enough to draw unwanted attention in their direction, and it gave him precious time to think. Manfred was conscious that the dogs and men, who he rightly suspected were not just hunters or poachers as Lukós had said, but something much worse were closing in on their position. He assumed, rightly, they'd been betrayed by someone and the Germans were searching the forest looking for them.

Always best to assume the worst, had been part and parcel of his military training.

He had to think fast. He had no idea which way to move. Using the girl they could try and retrace their steps to the farm and the relative safety of the barn, but there was no saying that by now the farm, the barn and the surrounding land wasn't already overrun with troops. He could not let them be captured, not now. Not having got this far. But he was wise to the Nazi ways and it was obvious they would search the area until they found who they were looking for. Manfred was single minded, focused and dispassionate enough not to consider the lives of the innocent that could get caught up in all this. Like the girl, standing rubbing her eyes and sniffling, or her family.

He had to decide and decide fast. There was no time to waver. He could make the girl keep taking them in the same direction towards the pass, and try and dodge and hide in the undergrowth the oncoming search party. But that was risky. The dogs would quickly pick up their scent long before the men caught up with them. Ultimate surrender and capture was not something the soldier contemplated.

To turn right and try and find an alternative without a knowledgeable person showing the way, could also be a big mistake. To go 'blind' would almost certainly lead them straight to the enemy or too close to the Nazi's sprawling army barracks that straddled the hills to the north.

No way ahead or taking a blundering route to the right.

Keep moving left. That was the only plausible move.

He glanced towards the trees. In the gloom of the all encompassing forest, it appeared an even thicker wall of closely packed trees and bushes. Nothing had forced their way through for a long time, it was unyielding and dense.

'Do you know if there's a way to get through there?' he asked the sniffling Teresa. She was sulking. This man had shouted at her and she didn't like him. She wanted to go home to *Mutti*.

The dogs were frighteningly close by now.

'Tell me. Do you know?' he snarled through clenched teeth.

She shrugged noncommittal and rubbed at her nose that was running. *Mutti* would want to know why she'd not used her hanky, but she thought she must have lost it somewhere.

'Tell me.' He was getting frustrated and desperate. Why had he let them talk him into trusted this child who to him seemed dull-witted. His mission had been to safe the important young woman and it seemed he might yet fail. What would happen to his ward and the maid, if they were caught? He couldn't, wouldn't think of the consequences. They were running out of time.

'I might. If you go that way it's not as far to a road that the German's use for their trucks and cars. I've seen them through the trees.'

He was thinking fast.

141

'Are you sure?' he insisted. 'There's a road just through the trees? How far to get to this road?'

Teresa shrugged again, but not having any idea of distance or time said, 'Not very far.'

She remembered how, one day, she'd wandered of her usual path chasing after a rabbit that had disappeared into the undergrowth. It was close by where they were now, because she was almost sure she recognized the dirt filled rabbit hole in the hump of earth to their right. She'd ventured in, parting the thick bushes and, the rabbit long forgotten, had suddenly heard the rumble of vehicle's engines. She'd curiously followed the sound, suddenly the trees had thinned and she found herself standing, hiding behind the last of the trees, watching as army vehicle after vehicle rolled past going north. So many she lost count.

Teresa had found her way back to the path she knew, and had not ventured that far again. She was sure this was the place, and that tiny gap in the trees to her left would be the way back to the road, and she said so.

'Right,' the man called Manfred spoke to them. 'This is what we do. Lukós and I will circle round to the right and try to cause a diversion. We'll be down wind to the dogs so hopefully we'll surprise them before they get the scent.'

He was talking to Brigitta and Viktor now, ignoring the girl as she peered with renewed confidence into the thicket.

'You go with the girl and pray she can take you to this road she mentioned. Keep moving forward as best you can. If you hear anything suspicious, or other than my signal whistle, hide and keep very very quiet and still. Understand?'

The woman nodded.

'Keep alert. Make for the opening to the road but stay hidden just inside the bordering line of trees. Keep the torchlight pointing down. We'll meet up with you once we've got the dogs off the trail.'

142

Before they had chance to question his plan, he handed the woman his torch. Without another word the men took off in the general direction of the baying dogs. Almost immediately they disappeared into the forest.

'Come,' Brigitta was ordering her son and Teresa, and without a word, the three made for the cover of the trees to the left.

Teresa pushed her way ahead confident she knew the way through, although she been this way only once.

With the two following close, and the round torch beam, she navigated her way through the thickets clothed already in buds and so tall they bent in places like an arch overhead. Once she stopped to get her bearings, and Brigitta trampled the clump of nettles and bracken with her boots to make it easier for the youth to pass.

Brambles clawed at their faces. Low level branches whipped against their bodies as they faltered and then moved on.

A dead end. A wall of matted, thorn-covered limbs so dense not even a small rodent could get through its impenetrable mass. Teresa stood for a second, hands on her hips, then without waiting for the others, sidestepped the bush and squeezed through the narrow gap between two massive pines.

Underfoot, their boots made satisfactory crunching and crackling sounds as they struggled across the dry, dead leaves of ages.

The three stopped once more, holding their breath and listened as behind them shots rang out.

Once, twice. How close? The gunfire was muffled with the compacted vegetation all around, but the sound spurred them on.

They hadn't spoken since they separated from the men, but the youth suddenly let out a yell. The trees ahead had started to thin, the younger trunks were sparse and well-spaced. The navy sky, with the fast dissolving cover of clouds, was suddenly revealed.

In his eagerness to get out of the claustrophobic scene, the youth tumbled and his mother caught him before he fell, but still displaced his hat with the brim pulled down over his face. It fell and caught on some brambles, but it revealed a cascade of rich, black hair that fell to the beautiful young woman's shoulders.

Manfred and Lukós, the two ex Hungarian Second Army soldiers moved swiftly and silently through the trees. They were professionals, well trained and very able. Manfred and Lukós, guns at the ready knew something of the art of jungle warfare and without the others hindering them they quickly fell into semi-crouching, ultra-alert movements towards the direction of the howling, barking dogs. Their own safety was unimportant. The foe was very close, and it was down to the two men to draw them away from the two escaping to the west.

Just ahead they heard shouts and a gun was fired indiscriminately. The dogs howled with tethered frustration. They'd picked up a scent and wanted to run free. Manfred, the leader, indicated they would split up and in a pincer movement try and get around the immediate threat, and with an element of surprise beat them at their own game.

The two women and the little girl exited the forest and found themselves at the edge of the road side. At this time of night it was unlit, because of possible air attacks, and empty of traffic. It was little more than a narrow dirt track, but made wider to accommodate the heavy army trucks and jeeps that travelled it, in single file, either to or from the Army barracks close by.

The two women sat on a small knoll of grass and the younger unused as she was to physical activity of any sort, bent double to ease the sharp pain in her side.

144

Teresa stood just inside the tree line and stared. It was almost unbelievable that the youth, thin and gaunt in a jacket and trouser too big for his small frame, was this girl. She couldn't stop staring openmouthed. She was like a princess.

The old woman glancing up, remonstrated harshly.

'Don't stare girl,' she said. 'Don't you know it's rude to stare.'

More harshly than was necessary, her words were vitriolic and lacking in warmth. She was thankful to be free at last of the tension and danger that had gripped her for so long, but now the danger wasn't immediate she couldn't stem her high born opinion or that she considered Teresa of such a low status she was little better than one of the farm animals that had roamed the many acres of the chateau. What was worse, and probably made her more unfeeling, was the sense neither her mistress nor herself would ever be able to return to their beloved Hungary. These thoughts made her sharp, and cruel towards the child.

Teresa was unhappy and confused. She didn't like these people her mother had said needed their help. They were unkind and she took a few steps away, turning her back so she didn't have to look at them.

It was dark and very dark trying to peer back into the heart of the forest. She turned so she could gaze towards the point where she could just make out in the dark, the ribbon of road disappearing into the blackness. The whole area looked so different and unrecognizable from her earlier visit. The sky had cleared of the clouds and a sudden beam of moonlight highlighted the road, bordered on both sides by scrubland and woods. On their side the line of the forest, alongside the road, stretched for quite a distance until it disappeared around a natural outcrop of fallen rocks.

No one spoke as they caught their breath and rested for awhile. The older woman heaved the carpet bag she had been carrying all the journey, never allowing it to be out of

145

her possession for a moment, and undid the clasp. She lifted out the packets of homemade cheese and course bread Hilde had provided, hardly able to hide her contempt at the free food. Ignoring Teresa she offered it to the young woman who delicately nibbled at a small piece, then with sublime delicacy dabbed at her mouth with the proffered wisp of lace.

Teresa watched in a mixture of awe and dislike, thinking, 'I don't want any, anyway,' as she deliberately forgotten. She shrugged her shoulders and found the two biscuits Hilde had wrapped and put in the pocket of her coat.

The truth was Teresa was feeling very tired, more than hungry, and she wanted more than anything to be home again in her bed, safe and sound.

Suddenly in the distance they heard a volley of rapid gunfire that made all three jump and the woman, with surprising agility, sprang to her feet and pulled the other into the shelter of the trees to one side of Teresa.

Teresa chest heaved with fright and tears rolled down her cheeks. She sniffed and shook with fear. She wanted *Mutti*. She didn't want to be here with these people. They didn't care about her. Not like her mother and father.

'What shall we do?' the young woman had hardly spoken a word during the entire race through the trees, was clinging to the woman who patted her arm as if to calm a small frightened child.

'We wait. Manfred and Lukós will come for us,' Brigitta sounded more confident than she felt.

It was working. The sounds of the German's boots trampling and crushing dried and brittle vegetation, along with the shuffling and growls from the dogs, meant they were close. Lukós, circling to the right, was unsure as to the exact location of Manfred, but supremely confident their leader was where he believed he'd be: to the left of his own position and marginally in front, between him and the enemy. He hid behind a tree and using only touch, rechecked the rounds of ammo in his handgun. They both had extra bullets in their pockets when and if needs be.

A low, almost illegible, whistle told him Manfred was in position and he stepped from the safety of the tree and moved stealth fully, doubled over towards the dip between two ancient trees. The dogs barked with growing excitement. Lukós could just see the shadowy form of Manfred dashing forwards towards the dogs and their handlers. He stopped and rustled the bush at his side causing enough of a sound to attract the men and dogs and now, in the twilight and shade, they could clearly make out the outlines of their adversaries.

No time to think.

Lukós stepped out from behind a tree, took aim and fired once, twice. His first bullet hit a soldier in the centre of his chest and he clutched at the wound before falling back, dead.

The dogs, quickly set loose, rushed into the trees setting up a collective ferocious howling and snarling as they sensed their prey.

Two of the Germans sprang away from their former position, rifles pointing forward and sending a volley into the trees. Splattered wood and bark threw in all direction as the soldiers, stepping over their dead comrade sent a more bullets into empty space. The dogs had found Manfred and stood snarling, uncertain waiting for orders from their handlers', but their prey took aim, and fired. Two of the blood hounds were dead within seconds. Lukós coming fast from the shelter of the trees to Manfred's left finished off the last two with fatal shots.

One dog suddenly bounded out and was hit mid leap, dead before it hit the ground. The soldiers weren't far behind the dogs, following the gunfire and now they were firing wildly at anything they thought was a target. The forest was so dense at this position that it was impossible to see what they were firing at, as slithers of tree bark and

147

branches were sprayed and bullets ricochet off tree trunk in every direction.

Lukós winced as a large splinter embedded itself in his cheek, and he hastily wiped away the blood flowing down his chin.

The Hungarians were moving swiftly now, as near to the ground as they could be and darting from the shelter of one tree to the next so they were hard targets to aim at. The cloak of the night forest, made it harder for the less experienced young German's to hit anything other than trees. Another soldier died and Manfred shot another as he faced him eye to eye.

Now the dogs were not longer a threat, it was easy for Manfred and Lukós, amid the general confusion of the battle to backtrack. Silently and with experience together now, they disappeared back into the thickest part of the forest. Taking the risk they had judged it to be right path, they headed north taking the route through the substantial trees that would ultimately lead them to the road.

Manfred hoped the others had found the edge of the forest and were now waiting for them. He was thinking on his feet: first get as much distance between them and what was left of the patrol and worry about what to do when they met up with the women. He hoped that he had gauged it just right and he would come close to leaving the forest in the same place they had.

Lukós didn't comment, trusting as always in Manfred, but he knew they had made themselves known to the enemy, by killing the dogs and at least two of the men, and the German's would be after them in force.

'I think we've lost them,' he whispered as the dense trees thinned out, giving way to the smooth surface of the moonlit road.

Manfred didn't reply.

They followed the road jogging evenly, but keeping close to the cover of the forest. They must have gone for a half mile or so, hoping all the time they hadn't misjudged the distance and missed the maid and the young woman. Then they saw them standing just in the shadow of the trees.

'Thank God,' the women cried with relief when she saw them coming. She didn't want to know what the gunshots were about or if anyone had been hit or died. Their two soldier escorts were here, fit and well and that was all that matter. She took a piece of cloth from her bag and busied herself dabbing at the cut on Lukós's face until he irritated pushed the old woman's hand away. It was nothing and he didn't need this fuss. Anyway he rather hoped he would have a scar to show of this fight.

'What do we do now?' he asked.' The sun will be up in a couple of hours and we don't want to be so conspicuous.'

Manfred nodded. He was thinking of their next move. He knew there would be more soldiers out looking for them, probably blanketing the whole area and making it impossible to work their way back to the crossing point that would take them over the border. Their only option was to keep moving, using the close-knit trees for as much cover as possible and once passed the forest to find empty building, barns, hills more woods anything that could give them hiding places so that gradually they could make their way to the Italian border. He explained his plan.

'But the Italian's would only arrest us and probably hand us over to the SS,' argued Lukós.

'But it might be our only chance to escape. Staying here and fighting would be suicide and we couldn't hope to go back and to cross the border to Switzerland now.'

They stood and pondered for as long as Manfred was willing to give them. It was his plan and it was the best plan, he just had to think on his feet. Whatever happened he would get them to safety or die trying.

'What about her?' They all turned to look at the little girl standing just outside their group. Teresa had been listening and yawning. Her legs ached, her feet ached and she rubbed constantly at her eyes with the knuckles of both hands.

Manfred had all but forgotten their young guide. If he was honest, now out of the forest, she was one more problem he didn't need.

Just another problem, but still a child and alone. He refused to think of her as his responsibility.

'Do you know your way back to your home?' Brigitta asked.

Teresa yawned deeply and shrugged her shoulders.

'We can't just leave her here,' Lukós remarked stating the obvious. If truth be known and he wasn't about to admit the fact: he'd not wanted to rely so heavily on a child in the first place. Now she was little more than a liability.

'If she's picked up by the German's she tell them everything about us. She knows we are going to try for the Italian border.'

Manfred gave an exasperated shrug. 'So what would you suggest we do?' He wanted them to move off now. There was still so much danger in this area.

'We'll have to take her with us,' answered the woman succinctly..

'No. I don't think that's the answer' said Manfred unable to hide his surprise at this suggestion. What on earth would they do with her? She would only hold them back, and probably make a fuss.

'No,' Teresa had found her voice. 'I don't want to go with you. I want to go home to *Vater und Mutti und* Leisl.' She stamped her foot and her mouth opened in a high pitched sob. They were discussing her as if she couldn't hear them.

'I want to go home.'

Her wails seemed so loud in the absolute stillness of the night and Manfred wondered how far noise carried. The possibility of being heard and bringing the patrols to their present vicinity, was a constant at the front of his mind.

'Quiet,' Manfred growled moving closer towards her, a move that only frightened the little girl even more.

'You will come with us, like a good girl. We'll think of a way to get you back to your family. But you must come with us now before the before the German's move in.'

'NO.'

Her mouth was open wide, and saliva, tears mixed with the mucus pouring from her nose spread across her cheeks. She rubbed at her face until it was smeared in the mess.

Even as tired as she was, before anyone could stop her, Teresa turned and took off back between the pines. Within seconds she had completely disappeared, swallowed up by the dark, unforgiving undergrowth.

'Quick after her,' ordered Manfred.

Lukós made to follow but stopped for only the first time disobeying his commanding officer. It was not his job to chase after a child and if they did as Brigitta suggested and take her along, what would that achieve? The girl would just be a small, unwelcome burden and probably more trouble that she was worth.

And if he followed orders and chased after her into the forest, there was the real possibility of becoming disorientated and lost. No. Let the girl take her chance.

It was Brigitta who spoke his thoughts.

'Leave her be. She'll find her way home a wild child of the forest.'

Manfred didn't pause for thought. It seemed fate had taken charge and made the decision for him. The old woman spoke the truth. The girl had been of use, but now she was on her own.

A child of the forest.

Silently, and without a backwards glance the men, and the women they'd vowed to protect at all cost, set off towards the Italian border.

Teresa ran and ran between the trees. Was that man following her, chasing after her? She tripped over a piece of uneven ground and stopping herself from pitching forward into a bank of thorns, grabbed at a small sapling struggling to find space amongst its elders. She steadied herself and looked about and the as ever the forest, on all sides, seemed to close around her like a suffocating cloak. She was standing on the cushiony mound of moss in the centre of a small, shallow unfamiliar clearing.

Chewing thoughtfully on her bottom lips, she turned slowly on the spot. If she could just see a tree or a stump or a bush she knew, and would direct her in the way back home, but it was dark and unyielding. The forest was so big and the recognizable part, she knew for certain, was only a very small part. She had no idea which way to go next.

Teresa was lost.

The sudden scurrying of a woodland creature close to her feet startled her, making her hop from one foot to the other.

The presence of the unseen animal had her rooted to the spot, unable to move. She was terrified and more sobs caught in her throat. She was all alone and very scared, but unconsciously she grabbed the two items around her neck held them tight.

'Remember Teresa,' her mother had said. 'Baby Jesus will take care of you. Pray *my liebchen.*'

The beads of the rosary and the chain holding the crucifix, bit into her small palm but it was a comforting feeling, not at all a hurting one.

Something else was quite close to the small clearing. She could hear it snuffling about and smell its body heat. There was movement in the bush at her side and the stems with ripe new growth shivered. The way the animal seemed to blunder through the nearby bush meant it was probably large. Or it might be Lukós searching for her, or even one of the men with dogs and guns. She didn't wait to find out. Teresa pushed and fought her way through the undergrowth in front of her and kept going until she couldn't go any further.

She stopped again, now so very tired she rubbed her eyes with her knuckles. She must get home and without thinking if it was the right way or not, or even if she would find herself back on the road, she ran into the thicket to her right.

Hilde was beside herself with worry. What had she done? She had put her own daughter in danger.

The last person she wanted in her home, telling her it was the right thing to do, and she was sure as sure she could be that Teresa would be fine, was Lotti Hofler. Hilde had never been argumentative or confrontational, if anything she was someone who had always done as she was told without too much opposition. But this was too much to ask any mother who had not only just lost her unborn, but knowingly put her small daughter at risk. What was she thinking? This wasn't some sort of game, this was very real.

'Get out Lotti,' she'd quietly demanded when the other woman started fussing around her and constantly repeating that everything would be fine, like a monotonous mantra until Hilde couldn't take it anymore. 'How can you know that for sure? Leave me alone.'

After the woman, with an indignant scowl had walked through the door, and moments later the car could be heard roaring away like a wounded bear, Hilde sat at the large pine table, her head resting on her forearm. Her eyes were dry and gritty, her throat parched and raw with crying and keening.

She still felt weak but she had to go out and search the forest. She couldn't sit and do nothing knowing Teresa might already have been captured and taken away. In her mind's eye she imagined the small, frightened figure being marched between two huge, bullying German's to a fate Hilde simply refused to envisage. Or they might just shoot her dead, without any more consideration than putting down a rabid dog. She didn't include the refugees in her thoughts. Now, right now, their fate meant nothing to this mother out of her mind with worry. She blamed them, it was the fault of the two strong fearless bodyguards and their charges.

Who were they? She didn't know.

Royalty or beggars? She didn't much care.

And with uncharacteristic venom she blamed the Hoflers for daring to put her child at risk, while their own daughter was safe and sound, asleep in her bed. But most of all she blamed herself for her weakness, in being persuaded to sacrifice Teresa.

Hilde raised her head and her eyes flicked to the book on the top of the dresser. With a heavy heart, dizzy and light headed and limbs that refused to move quickly, she picked up the book and found the passage she needed to read more than anything.

Psalm 37 verse 39
'But the salvation of the righteous is of the Lord. He is their strength in the times of trouble. And the Lord shall help them: shall deliver them from the evil ones and save them because they trust him.'

The words held hope and comfort, and she read the passage again and again then offered a prayer to the Lord for the safe return of her daughter.

Teresa felt her way in the dark. She clung to the short, whipping branches low down and winced when her hand closed on branches full of thorns. It felt more and more as if the packed, spiky bushes seemed to reach out on purpose and grab at her clothes. Her face and hands were scratched and bleeding, with trying to push her way through the unforgiving tangle of bracken. She hurt everywhere and, try as she might, couldn't stop crying.

She was so frightened.

'Baby Jesus please, please help me to get out of the forest and back home to my *Mutti* and *Vater*, and sister Leisl. I promise I'll be a good girl forever, and never pinched my sister's arm when she tells on me,' she whispered between the sobs that hurt her chest and throat. A rustling very close behind, spurred her on. The men with the guns were coming after her.

One more clump of thick bushes and close tree trunks, more obstacles, and Teresa with the last of her strength pushed her way through.

Instead of the crisp forest floor she now stepped onto what was a dried bed of a steam. For the first time she realized just how thirsty she was, and wished there had been at least a trickle left for her to drink.

Across the narrow gap and she was at the foot of a slight rise that rose up the side of a low hillock. Around her now, the trees were thinning and the few growing along the top of the ridge were deciduous only just acquiring their spring clothing.

Here through the sparse overhead canopy she was able to see pieces of the sky and a smattering of stars.

Wearily Teresa she struggled and scrambled up the side of the hill and with the aid of an exposed root, growing out through the tangled weeds, pulled herself to the top.

Even in the semi light she could make out the treeless pasture with rolling hills beyond. From the bottom of the hill the ground stretched away in a strange colourless tapestry to blend seamlessly with the distance shapeless forms of higher hills and mountains. These covered the horizon from right to left.

Even now, with one hand held to her face to try and accentuate her vision, she imagined she could see a scatterings of white dots that indicated roaming farm animals, sheep or goats.

At the foot of her hill, the foreground held more clusters of shrubs and stubby trees no more than shadowy, mounds reminiscent of large animals crouching ready to pounce on the unsuspecting.

Up on the hill it was very cold and a strong breeze blew from the east. Teresa shivered until her teeth chattered. She started down, sliding and falling until she hit the bottom with a thump that left her breathless and bruised.

She looked about her eager to find a landmark she recognized.

Where was she? Where was her family? She was so scared, that suddenly her legs gave from under her and she sat down on the hard ground right beside a tall, solitary tree. It wasn't much but it did offer her some protection from the strengthening wind. For what seemed ages to the child, but was only a matter of minutes, she rested her back against the rough bark and looked out to the open plain. She wished she was home in her bed she shared with Leisl and she gave one single sob before she yawned deep and long. She could hardly keep her eyes open a minute longer.

Something had woken her, and for a moment she struggled to remember where she was. This wasn't the bed in the roof space. It was hard and uncomfortable and bits of twigs and dead leaves were sticking into her flesh.

She sat up, suddenly alert to the sounds. To men's voices, calling loudly and very near, followed by what sounded like thrashing about amongst the bushes. They were close to finding her hiding beneath the tree. In a terrified panic Teresa sprang to her feet. She knew instinctively these men were not her friends and she ran.

Across the pasture and towards the gentle slope of a hill opposite. Not once did she glance back to see if she was being followed, but the sounds of the men faded as she left behind the ridge of the hill and the forest beyond.

She kept running. Her legs ached but she kept going, never doubting in her young mind she might be going in the wrong direction. Over the clover-choked wild grasses and sweet smelling meadow lilies. Creeping, unseen roots and vines grabbed at her boots and more than once she tripped and fell, but quickly got back to her feet. Teresa didn't notice the pain in her knee or the speckles of blood on her stockings until she collapsed out of breath and lay back amongst the wildflowers. Then back again on her feet.

She'd grazed her knee, but she had no time to think about it as she kept running towards the rolling hills that now had the crested hint of the dawn: no more than a fine golden line on the horizon. She had no idea where she was, or where she was going: she just knew she had to keep running.

At last she could go no further, and slumped down, lying flat on her back. She was, again, out of breath and her sobs caught in her throat as she gulped in the clear mountain air. She was so tired and hungry, and her knee really hurt. She looked down at it and cried even harder at the sight of the blood that had dried and now stained her stocking a dirty brown.

Slowly, very slowly she got back to her feet. She didn't want to, but she made herself look back the way she'd come in case the men were following her. It was a long way away, so far away she could hardly make out the tops of the pine trees that formed the beginning of the forest. They were such a distance they were almost hidden by the hills between.

There wasn't a sound or movement. It was so silent she could hear her belly rumbling. The sudden shimmering arc of light grew stronger, hovering above the rim of the distance hills and heralding the dawn. Without warning the chorus began with the flurry of wings and a bird flying from

157

its well-hidden ground nest. It had been so close to the unsuspecting girl that she jumped violently.

Then she ran.

She was stumbling with sheer weariness when she lifted her head to peer at the hills in front of her. The sun was getting higher in the clear blue sky, and the air was filled with the intoxicating scents of Alpine plants, pine and earthy bracken.

She fought her way to the top of the hill higher than the previous one. She could hardly keep her eyes open and she didn't think she could go any further. With eyelids half closing so her lashes swept the fine down of her cheeks, she stood swaying and looked out to the next part of her journey. But there was something familiar, jutting out like a sentinel, above the slope of the next rise. Teresa's heart leapt in her chest.

She thought she recognized it.

For the hundredth time, Teresa prayed, holding tightly the objects around her neck. Tears now streaked and dried on her cheeks, she wiped away the last of the damp from her eyes so she could see clearly and make absolute sure she wasn't imagining it.

Quickly now and oblivious to the skid and tumbles on her descent she rushed down , across the small valley and up the rise.

The object she had fixed her gaze on became ever clearer as she neared the top and suddenly reaching the top, the landscape opened up again to panorama of pastures and undulating hills. In the valley could be seen the outline of steeple on the top of the tiny church. The same church she attended almost daily. If she stood for a moment and looked to the right of the church steeple she could just make out the tops of buildings, the school house and in the distance the clock tower of the town hall.

All so familiar: she was home.

Chapter 15

Teresa Hunt, sitting alone in her adopted country on Remembrance Day seventy years later, recalled it all as if it had happened yesterday.

She'd run the rest of the way home that morning. Even in the chill of an early morning her mother had been sitting outside the door, on the three-legged stool her father had made. She been looking very sad her face turned towards the forest in the distance. She didn't see her daughter until Teresa yelled, '*Mutti. Mutti.*'

Hilde sprang up from the stool knocking it over and scattering the hens that had been scratching about in the dirt at her feet. She looked pale and thin, and sick but she ran to Teresa and gathered her up in her arms, hugging her so tight Teresa thought she might be squashed, but not caring one bit. It was good to be home and safe in her mother's arms. This time her mother didn't scold or shout, but she cried and that made Teresa cry until they were sobbing together.

Teresa was surprised it wasn't even breakfast time.

'I must get ready for school,' she yawned and rubbed her eyes as Hilde prepared a large creamy bowl of porridge and placed it on the pine table before her daughter. She couldn't resist putting her arms around Teresa and giving her another long hug. She had been so worried and the long hours had stretched out through the night only broken by the return of Josef who after the evening of strong wine had fallen asleep in his clothes. Hilde hadn't bothered to wake him, it was better that way. All night she'd sat and waited, unsure what to do for the best, but her growing fear turning her insides to a churning mass.

Even before the first light, Hilde had taken the stool and sat outside hardly noticing the chill that soaked through thin clothing to her skin. Occasionally she stood, and on stiffening limbs had walked across the meadow to the forest, but always stopping before the perimeter. It was hopeless to think she could locate her daughter in its dark, menacing depths. Even from a distance she could hear the activity of the searchers and the barking tracker dogs. Her heart had beat fast, and with a growing sense of dread and hopelessness she'd walked slowly back to take up her vigilance on the stool. She'd prayed and prayed until she was sure God must be sick of hearing her pleading.

Hilde had thought her heart would stop its feeble beating when she heard Teresa's voice. Her daughter safe and sound, she mouthed again and again her silent prayer of thanks. She promised, that because her prayers had been answered she would continue to thank him 'til her dying day.

'No. Not today, *leibchen*. Today you stay home and rest.'

Teresa gave that some thought as she ate hungrily the food in the bowl and emptied the glass of the fresh goat's milk. For once *Mutti* didn't get angry when she rushed her food, and even refilled the bowl with more.

'What will Fraülein Weisz say if I'm off school?' she muttered her words slurred with tiredness. 'And *Vater*, he will be so cross if I miss my lessons?' but it was hard to keep her eyes open a second longer.

For four days and nights, the German's patrolled the huge, sprawling pine forest to the southwest of the town. In the town itself certain people of interest or suspected of helping the murderers of the two soldiers and the gunshot wounding of a third, were rounded up and herded off to the barracks for interrogation. The once relative peaceful cohabitation between the Austrians and their German invaders had come to an end. Many on both sides were wary of neighbours and previous friends. Who could they trust now not to spy on them or report them for whatever reason? It was a strange and unnerving situation.

Only the mayor and police chief Herr Heinrich Mueller were exempt from any suspicions, as he watched and seemed to applaud the rough handling of the men and women now from the soldiers. He didn't flinch when Bernard Fischer, the boy in his late teens and given to harmless mischief-making argued with the German sergeant over who had thrown an over ripe tomato and only missing the soldier by a small margin. To the shock of the townspeople going about their business, they had to stand and stare as the boy was hit repeatedly over the head with the butt of the sergeant's rifle, until he lay senseless and badly hurt.

This was only one of the cruel punishments metered out by the angry soldiers and often in the square, outside the townhall and in full view of Mueller. He sat, amused and watchful, seated behind the desk strategically placed in the office window. He never missed anything.

Suddenly people were scared of their own shadows.

As the weeks and months went on the intimidation and terror lessened, but there was no more than an uneasy peace and closeted resentment from that time on. Now there was no friendly co-operation on either side.

Just as they thought it was over and nothing more could affect the small community, the wounded soldier died of his injuries six weeks later and the unrelenting terror and doubt started again.

It was on an evening when the light was fading but what was left of the sunlight covered the ground outside the house with a silvery glow, that the Göetschl family, seated around the large, well-scrubbed pine table eating a meal of meat and dumplings, heard a vehicle draw up outside. It stopped with a screech of brakes and squeal of heavy tyres and the clang of a tailgate being lowered.

Teresa sprang from the table, followed closely by Leisl and ran to gaze outside the window at the army lorry disgorging the five soldiers. If she'd been traumatized by her own experience she didn't show it. In fact the child was happy and bright as she'd ever been and for that Hilde had been thankful. Perhaps, as she'd hoped, Teresa viewed it as an adventure and nothing more, but she kept her promise and never spoke of it.

Hilde and Josef both rose to their feet to see what all the commotion was about, and Teresa stepped away from the window as the men rushed towards the door. She gripped her hands together at her chest, breathing hard and with a tremble in her small body. Men with guns. Suddenly she felt very afraid and ran to cling to her mother legs, burying her face in her mother's skirt. It hadn't gone unnoticed by her mother that since the incident Teresa had become more reserved and thoughtful. It saddened Hilde that her former bubbly, happy child had forgotten how to laugh.

Before her father could reach the door, it was forced open breaking the inside bolt and almost taking it off its stout hinges. The men were inside their home, and the room felt smaller. They raised their rifles and aimed them at the family. Leisl, now under the table clutching her doll was crying loudly as Teresa whimpered into Hilde's skirt.

'What do you want?' Josef tried to sound forceful but he knew it didn't sound convincing. 'How dare you break into my house. Your Commandant, a friend of mine, will hear of this despicable behaviour.'

The men ignored him. They didn't care.

'You are to come with us,' ordered the one who looked the most senior and intimidating.

The family could do nothing. No amount of anger, cajoling or pleading worked and to the dismay of his wife and children Josef Gőetschl was thrown into the back of lorry, the soldiers climbed in after him and with a mighty roar of its engine, it drove off at speed.

All that night Hilde, unable to get any sleep, worried and fretting about the fate of her husband. Why? Why had the Nazi's taken him? Josef of all people was as loyal to Hitler and the Party as any member of the Reich. Why had they suddenly turned upon him? She was frantic to know and this was the question Hilde asked Heinrich Mueller as soon as she'd left the girls at school the following morning and walked to the offices of the unelected mayor.

The plump, officious man leaned back in his leather office chair so he could get a better look at the woman standing before him and locked his fingers behind his head. Hilde was looking indignant and worried, but desirable.

Even though with everything that had happened she had lost weight, so her normal shapely figure did not fill her clothes in the way he so admired, she was still a beautiful woman. He hardly noticed now her eyes were dulled and the usual rose-blush in her cheeks was sadly missing. Of course he'd heard about her recent indisposition, he knew about everything that went on in his town, but that was women's problems. He contemplated this possible opportunity before him, she still made the blood rush in his veins and his desire had not diminished. If he locked the office door, maybe she would provide a service right here and now?

'Hilde this is a pleasure ---,' he beamed without given anything of his true thought away.

'Why have they taken Josef,' she interrupted him before he could continue his spiel. She could almost read his mind and her contempt for him threatened to overshadow her reason for being there.

'If anyone knows what's happening you do,' she snapped pointing an angry finger.

The plump mayor relaxed his arms and sat up in his chair. He was unfazed by her sharpness. He was the mayor, the police chief and confidante of the most important person in the town, so he was supremely superior to this woman standing before him, demanding answers, when all he wanted to do was rip her clothes off.

'I only know what my good friend the Oberführer has told me,' he answered a smile, more of a sneer, on his face.

'You see,' he continued, 'he is far from a happy man. Three of his soldiers are now dead, killed at the hands of terrorists trying to escape through the forest near your land.'

For one horrible minute Hilde felt her expression might give her away, her expression of horror, betray her. She fought down the waves of dizziness and hoped her next words would sound normal.

'Yes. Yes. I know the Germans have been searching the forest and around our place for days looking for these people,' she answered quickly and with growing impatience. 'I know all that. I also know no one was found, as it's rumoured they probably escaped over the border. But you haven't answered my question. Why have they arrested my husband, and what are they doing to him?' she was wringing her hands with a mix of frustration and fear.

He brought his shoulders up into his neck as a shrug, and placed his hands palms up, on his desk. For an instance he seemed reluctant to say more, but her expression made him add.

'It's like this Hilde. There has been certain whisperings and hints from – shall we call them 'informers'. They have implicated your husband in this treachery.'

Hilde gasped and clutched her chest as a sharp pain tore through her.

'That's ridiculous. Hasn't Josef always been a loyal supporter and friend to the Nazi's. You of all people ---.'

He flapped his hands as if indicating the sudden arrest of her husband was nothing to do with him, and in any case he didn't intend to get involved.

164

'I'm sorry Hilde, but you must see the problem here. This Jew had to have had help to get as far as they did. They were known to go into the forest and it is no surprise men and dogs were shot dead by these criminals. They were making for the Swiss border and somehow escaped. Thankfully that way has now been blocked from this side when Claus ordered it to be blown up. The avalanche of rocks and boulders means no one will get that way again.'

Hilde wasn't interested. She didn't care if the Germans had brought down a whole mountain. She wanted to know what they had done with her husband.

'But Josef's a sick man. You know that, Heinrich. It's a mistake --- a terrible mistake.' She was wracked with guilt. Josef was innocent.

She got no assistance from the mayor and was not allowed, by the Commandant, to see her husband held for interrogation, and it would be a further thirty six hours before Josef was finally released and returned to his family.

Chapter 16

Josef Gőetschl was a broken man. They had questioned him continually hour after hour, sometimes using mind games and often force. But how could he tell them what he didn't know? Eventually they'd pushed him out of the back of an army truck, into the centre of the square. His previous friends and comrades had betrayed him, he couldn't believe it, he was bewildered and Josef bitterly resented their allegations. No man had been so loyal.

Josef stopped walking into town to the Heurigen to drink the wine and chat with friends. The seizures became severe, and even the warmer weather that brought the first shoots of summer colour and fragrance in the meadows and hills surrounding the chalet, didn't brighten his moods. He was morose and depressed. He spent all his days in bed or sitting outside the home chipping away at pieces of wood, smoking, taking no interest in anything. He shook almost continually and very quickly the man in his mid thirties resembled someone twice his age. For a long time after his arrest he wore the bruises and cuts that covered a lot of his thin frame and he'd had two of his teeth knocked out. He would not talk or discuss his treatment at the hands of the people he'd once thought of as his comrades and friends, and he stubborn refused to answer any question Hilde asked.

As much as possible their parents kept the reason for his missing from the girls, but it was not surprising when Gunter Mueller jeered and taunted Teresa and Leisl about their father the traitor. That provoked Teresa to knock him to the ground and Leisl to burst into confused tears.

At the school, their teacher Fraülein Weisz obviously didn't believe their father's innocence and, annoyed at his release, continually picked on Teresa daily until the day she left to return to Salzburg in the summer of 44. Only Ingrid, her friend, stuck up for the unhappy little girl and stayed her one and only friend.

The weeks and months following Josef's arrest were hard. Hilde prayed for her husband's recovery and that everything would return to the way it was. But nothing did. It seemed their lives had changed forever, and his wife quietly watching him through the window, worried and prayed.

Josef was withdrawn, his life without any real purpose anymore and he seethed at the perceived injustice. Any life left was gradually draining from him leaving him a much troubled soul.

His seizures were more frequent, two or three a week, as if the trauma from his hours of incarceration and brutal treatment at the hands of the local Gestapo, had taken all his strength in his fight against the malaise.

The worry of almost losing her daughter and keeping her duplicity from her husband played on Hilde daily, and she spent more and more time on her knees in front of the altar in the church. Teresa even at seven understood something of where her father had been during his missing hours, but as he often spent time with his German friends she didn't question it. The majority of his injuries were hidden beneath his clothes, and the ones on show he insisted were the result of one of his seizures when he'd fallen heavily against furniture.

Leisl accepted the explanation and gently stroked his cheek.

'Poor Vater.'

Teresa didn't say anything but screwed her eyes up in a troubled frown.

Hilde prayed hard 'Hail Mary, Mother of God ---,' please don't let Teresa says anything. They were secrets so terrible, but how could she expect a seven year old child to keep quiet if, or when, she discovered the escaping Hungarians and her father's ill-treatment were connected? Sooner or later she would, Teresa was intelligent but precocious, and the child had suffered too, having spent an entire night in a forest, pursued and lost. Hilde worried at the problem. Teresa had promised her mother and Jesus she wouldn't tell anybody. Time and again Hilde had instilled in her the seriousness of this secret: to even let slip a word, would mean terrible consequences for so many people. People would get hurt and possibly even shot --- was this all too much of a burden to place on the shoulders of the little girl?

But she had made the promise and Teresa kept it safe and true for the next seventy years.

And it came as no surprise to Hilde that Teresa never went near the forest again, or that throughout her life Teresa suffered recurring dreams of isolation and dark, frightening confinement.

Josef, even after his wounds healed, lost interest in his Nazi's friends and their ideology. It hardly seemed of any importance anymore and in his darkest moods relished the growing possibility, as the raids on industrial cities became more intense, that the mighty Reich may not win after all. This he kept very much to himself, pretending he wasn't hurt or offended by his former friends blatant cold-shouldering the few times he did venture into the town. He knew there would always be many who believed he was guilty. Why else would they have arrested him? One of his old friends, Claude Schneider the butcher, was heard to remark, 'He must have had the devil himself on his side to get away with such a heinous crime against the state.'

The old woman, remembering, clicked her tongue against her teeth in disgust. 'Poor Vater he was so sad,' she muttered to a startled pigeon scratching at her feet.

Teresa and Leisl, apart from school and church, stayed at home. Only occasionally did Leisl still play with Connie and Tomas Schultz and rarely now did Teresa play with her best friend Ingrid Hofler. It seemed a particularly, unpleasant cloud had descended and the family grew more and more insular, and cut off from the rest of the townspeople.

Hilde was tired more often and her weight dropped drastically until her she seemed drawn and haggard with her bones sticking through her clothes. She found it an effort some morning to get up and make her daughter's breakfast before they went to church then on to school.

Doctor Brunner shook his head and scolded her in his aged, fatherly way, 'You have to rest more. Your heart has been weakened and the strain on it is not good.'

It helped her when Teresa did more of the housework and tended the small vegetable garden at the side of their chalet. Leisl took on the responsibility of feeding and caring for the goats, hens and the newly acquired pig. The small amount of sewing repairs or garments made, Hilde was starting to teach her two daughters the skills passed down from her mother and grandmother before her. Thankfully both were quick to learn, until their hand stitches were almost as perfectly as their mothers.

The hot summer went by relatively peacefully. Hilde saw Lotti Hofler only a few times after the incident, any earlier acquaintance forever tarnished. Hilde was glad of that. She preferred not to be reminded of how, not just herself, but her child had been implicated in the escape of someone deemed so important her own daughter's danger was insignificant. Hilde continued to resent the fact Lotti and Felix had apparently gone along with the mission while their own daughter was safe and sound in her bed. And then there had been the dreadful arrest of Josef, completely innocent. It was that which played so heavily on Hilde's conscience. Nor did she learn the identity of the young woman, dressed as a youth to escape and who had caused her own family so much heart break, and neither did she care.

The waves of Allied planes, American and British, flying overhead started that summer of 43. At first they were few crossing the mountainous region, surrounding the town squatting in the valley, turning north and on to bomb the factories in Steyr.

The activity in and around the town and the nearby barracks grew as more troops from Germany were marshaled. With the unerring assistance of Heinrich Mueller batteries of machineguns and anti-aircraft were quickly built on the surrounding hills. As the gentle heat of July turned to a scorching August, the bombing intensified. More planes droned overhead day and night making their way north to the marshaling yards in Vienna and the aircraft factories building Messerschmitt in Wiener Neustadt.

It was thrilling for Teresa and Leisl to watch out for the planes, and count the number in formation, not fully understanding the significance. Hilde called her daughter's to come inside, her fear of the mounting bombardment making her heart race. The world had gone mad. What was to become of them? What would happen to her beloved Austria? What if they dropped a bomb on their small house -- accidently or on purpose? These thought kept her awake at night beside the equally silent, and wakeful, Josef.

Her husband listened to another wave of planes flying over and felt nothing. No dread for what was happening to the cities in the north. No delight that the military that had taken over his country and who he'd trusted and supported was now being targeted. It meant nothing and he hardly listened to the propaganda news of never-ending German victory that issued daily from his wireless.

November 1943 a combined meeting of Britain, United States and the Soviet Union issued the Moscow

Declaration that declared to reinstate the Austrian state, free from the German rule, but that did not stop the country from being an enemy and so in December of that year, Innsbruck was targeted with such ferocity there was hardly a building left standing.

Josef wasn't interested.

It was in December of that year he caught a bad head cold. He stayed in bed, sneezing and coughing as his wife built up the fire and made him broth and tinctures of honey and herbs. Teresa and Leisl went each day to school, eagerly watching and waiting for the distant steady droning of aircraft and the intermittent rattle of machine guns from the anti-aircraft shelters. Hilde still managed to go to church each day to kneel and give thanks and ask for protection for the small community.

Although, with hardly any income, she paid for Doctor Brunner and the medicine. She nursed her husband as best she could not able to avoid his cold turning to bronchitis and then pneumonia. For days Josef, already weak, struggled to fight a raging fever and the convulsions that caused his slight body to heave and shake. A week later, during a strong *grande mal,* he finally lost the battle.

Hilde hated the Nazis. She blamed the Nazis.

On the day Josef died overwhelmed with grief and sudden uncontrollable anger, at the way her husband had been treated, she tore down from the wall facing their marriage bed-cupboard the last remaining icons. While alive, and even after what they'd done to him, he'd been loath to remove the Hitler photo and swastika flag but now, along with all her handmade armbands her family had been forced to wear, she burnt everything on the fire. With tears of grief she watched as the material smoldered, scorched and crumpled into black ash.

They were lovingly replaced by the Austrian flag, her grandmother's rosary and crucifix hanging on the peg on the wall and beside them her mother's picture of Our Lord on the cross.

Poor Vater. Poor Mutti!

In the winter of 1944/45 the air attacks on the industrial centres in and around the major cities intensified. March 1945 brought more Allied bombings of the oil refineries of Moosbierbaum, Schwechat, Korneuburg and Vienna, until on April 30th 1945 the USA troops entered Austria and the British and French followed soon after.

The German garrison outside the small town in the Tyrol put up a fight but soon surrendered and the Commandant Oberführer Schmit was arrested and taken away.

Hilde along with most of the townspeople watched in silence as he was loaded into the back of a US army lorry, alongside his lieutenants.

In shock and disbelief Heinrich Mueller watched through his office window. Only the day before he had bundled his wife and son off to Vienna and he intended to follow his family as soon as he could. The war was virtually over, and they'd lost.

But Mueller never left. On the very day, May 8th 1945 Germany surrendered and the Allies quickly began the job of rounding up the collaborators, Heinrich Mueller, self proclaimed mayor, police chief and SS Waffen, hanged himself from the clock tower at the top of the Rathaus.

Chapter 17

The aftermath of the war was felt around the globe. The world was broken and Hilde prayed daily that it could be mended for the sake of her children. Austria battered and bruised, had little to offer its citizens having to rely on the charity of other victorious nations to prove the essentials.

The British troops moved into Carinthia in 1945 and stayed ten years, it protected the country from the Communist threat surrounding it but also Austria was then a valuable resource for hard coal, and close to Vienna and Wolfsegg am Hausruck, oil and lignite.

1950

Hilde Gőetschl appeared to age almost overnight. She was too thin, and her once warm brown hair had turned white. Her eyes once the colour of chestnuts, were dim and lifeless as if her soul had already died. Her heart beat with a feeble irregularity as if it too was defeated with life.

Her daughters Teresa and Leisl were growing up fast. Teresa had turned fifteen in March and her sister thirteen the previous January. They spent long hours learning more of the dressmaking and seamstress skills passed on down the generations and soon both became as proficient as their mother.

The rolling hills and meadows were a painter's pallet of lush greens from the palest hint to the darkest tones, with polka dots of lazily grazing sheep, goats and cows. The musical sounds of cowbells, harmonized perfectly with the sound of birdsong high in the rich, deep blue of the cloudless sky. Vast carpets of wildflowers, in as many colour as the rainbow and more, stretched far to the horizon to meet dense, regimental forests and woodland clinging crazily to the hills and then on to the base of distant mountains. Crystal clear streams trickled and gurgled down the slopes as mini waterfalls, to join with the fast running rivers. In the valley the town and its people were gradually finding its way back from the horrors of war.

This was the Austrian Tyrol in summer.

It was such a beautiful morning and Hilde lingered for a time standing in her open doorway gazing out upon the scene before her. This was a picture she had lived with all her life and could not ever imagine living anywhere else.

Even after seven years she still mourned Josef and struggled almost daily with her loss: part of her raged at her God for taking him too soon, while she thanked him again and again for the years they'd had and for the gifts of her children. But her heart was broken, her life empty.

She leant against the door frame as the few hens, scratched and chuckled around her feet in the dry earth. Matilda the only goat left, scrambled up the side of a nearby hill and stood proudly on its summit. The once fertile vegetable garden, that had given them so much sustenance during the hard years, now had a sorry display of potatoes and carrot and cabbage greens, and very little else. The heart had gone out of the land.

Her daughters were at the market, seeing what they could afford and if anyone needed garments making or mending. But times were hard and it was unlikely they would find work.

Hilde sighed and turned to go back inside the cool and dim interior. Nothing much had changed over the years, the pine furniture, maybe more scratched and worn, was still solid and the log fire burnt bright even on such a day. Her worst moments were at night and the one side of the cupboard bed now empty. Maybe that was the reason she hardly slept anymore.

Without consciously doing it, she crossed to the wall and ran her fingers over the hanging chains of rosary and crucifix and looked again, as she had done more times than she could count, at the framed picture of the figure on the cross and the fragile face of the suffering Christ.

And as she had done daily since Josef's death she donned her coat and walked the short distance to the small church.

The inside was cool compared to the day's intense heat.

As usual the priest, Father Dominic greeted her with, 'Hello Frau Gőetchl, you are looking well.'

The priest still a young man, said the same greeting to all his parishioners whatever their age. It was recognised by all that social chitchat did not come easy to this ungainly, unworldly man of the cloth.

Hilde replied with her usual, 'Hello Father and you are looking well also,' and he made the sign of the cross in her general direction.

'Go with God', he muttered absentmindedly and scurried away perform one of his many pastoral duties.

The morning was the same as all the others. Father Dominic rushed off leaving Hilde her alone in the silent, peaceful world. She crossed herself and moved closer to gaze at the large carved statue above the altar, then moved backwards to sit on a front pew. It was this peace that above all else seemed to calm and sooth and she sat, her head bent in silent prayer.

It was so peaceful and restful, and she didn't want to move to get to her weary legs and walk the path home. Her heart seemed to race until she could feel the pulse throbbed in her the side of her neck, and her breathing slowed until her the rise and fall of her chest was barely noticeable. This place, this pew facing the figure on the cross and so close she could almost reach out and touch, felt strangely like home. Her limbs, her body relaxed and she listened for the sound of the voice. She smiled. It was a loving, gentle voice she recognized.

It was two hours later Father Dominic returned to find Hilde Gőetschl slumped sideways in the pew. Her tormented heart had finally stopped, and at last she was at peace.

Chapter 18

The old woman stood and gathered together the bags of shopping at her feet. She must get home. She was late and her neighbour would get shirty. *That word made her chuckle then she was serious. She shuffled along the path still reliving the past, the past she longed for, so she might forget the loneliness of the present. This country, this town, had been her home for so long that, sadly, much of her memories had faded.*

It had been so long ago.

The whole of Europe had been awash with refugees and displaced persons from many nations.

The following January the Austrian authorities together with a British delegation decided to resettle some of the young. They would all start new lives in other countries desperate for the skills lost amongst the dead of the war.

Teresa, always the outspoken, the protector of her sister, tried to object. They didn't want to leave Austria, their home, the little chalet on the side of the hill and move to a strange country they didn't know or understand the language. This argument only fell on deaf ears.

An English woman, dressed in foreboding grey, stood stolidly in front of the two girls. Her manner and forceful attitude reminded Teresa of Fraülein Weisz except this fraülein couldn't speak German and neither Teresa or Leisl understood her. But it soon became obvious that two young woman alone, with no family, had no more rights than many of the others. More objections, in German, from the determined Teresa and fearful tears from Leisl brought

179

hard slaps across their heads. They didn't understand a word, but understood this unexpected bullying.

'You should be grateful,' the woman in grey demanded with distain and dislike. 'After all you lost the war, and now *we* are having to give you new homes and work. You will do as you are told. You have no choice.' She ended this tirade with another couple of sharp slaps and a satisfactorily sneer aimed at the unfortunate sisters, and the state of the world in general.

It was a traumatic and sad departure the day Teresa and Leisl were put on the train that would take them to the enforced new life in England. As the train sped off leaving behind the clear air, the dipping valleys and the majestic beauty of the mountains, the tearful Teresa, two months away from her eighteenth birthday, knew she would never sec her beloved Austria again.

Footnote

Teresa and Leisl Gőetschl were resettled in Yorkshire to work in one of the cotton mills.

The sisters lived together in a small bedsit until the death of the younger sister Leisl, after contracting polio, less than a year later.

In 1953 Teresa married Yorkshire man Ernest Hunt a skilled weaver. The couple's only child, daughter Emily was born in 1954. Emily died in 1956 during a measles outbreak.

Teresa, with no other family, was left widowed and alone after forty years of happy marriage.

Their Jewish teacher Albert Grassinger and his elderly mother were listed as two of the victims of the gas chambers in Dachau.

There is no record of the fate of the Reiters, the young gypsy family with son Stefan, which had the small homestead in the next valley to the Gőetschls and mysterious disappeared one night.

Of the elderly couple the Wineburgs, on the run with the Szabó, and Mika and Yanni, Miriam Wineburg died on the way to find medical help and her husband arrested by the Nazi's didn't survive the concentration camp.

What happened to their travelling companions the two young men? It is assumed Yanni was shot dead and his friend Mika got across the border into Czechoslovakia. But as he was not heard of again and neither man carried identity or paper, the truth is unknown.

The Szabó family escaped over the mountain pass into Switzerland, and settled in Geneva. Their son David grew up to become the chairman of a leading bank.

There is still to this day a tale told in parts of Austria about a beautiful young Hungarian countess who, during the German occupation, disguised as a boy, Viktor and along with her maid Brigitta, and two brave soldier escorts fled to Austria and fought their way across the border into Italy. They eventually escaped on board a ship heading for America, and there they lived happy ever after. But as this is only folklore passed down the generations, no one can verify its authenticity. There was never any mention of a brave little girl who helped them.

It is possible the young woman lived for the rest of her life, unknown and unrecognized, amongst the New Yorkers and the soldiers escorts, Manfred and Lukós eventually went back to their homeland where both perished during the Hungarian Uprising of 1956.

Felix and Lotti Hofler with daughter Ingrid moved to a kibbutz in the newly former Israel in 1949 and never returned to the little town in Austria.

Table of Contents

www.ingramcontent.com/pod-product-compliance
Lightning Source LLC
Chambersburg PA
CBHW051122260626
47170CB00005B/1618